TERRITORY OF LIGHT

YUKO TSUSHIMA

TERRITORY OF LIGHT

Translated from the Japanese by Geraldine Harcourt

FARRAR, STRAUS AND GIROUX • NEW YORK

Farrar, Straus and Giroux
175 Varick Street, New York 10014

Printed in the United States of America
Originally published in Japan in 1979 by Kodansha Ltd., Japan, as *Hikari no Ryōbun*
English translation rights arranged with the Estate of Yuko Tsushima
    through Japan UNI Agency, Inc., Tokyo
English translation originally published in 2018 by Penguin Books Ltd.,
    Great Britain
Published in the United States by Farrar, Straus and Giroux
First American edition, 2019

The twelve chapters of this book first appeared as a story series in the literary
monthly *Gunzō* between July 1978 and June 1979.

Grateful acknowledgment is made for permission to reprint an excerpt from
Faust, by Johann Wolfgang von Goethe, translated by C. F. MacIntyre,
copyright © 1949 by New Directions Publishing Corp. Reprinted by
permission of New Directions Publishing Corp.

Library of Congress Cataloging-in-Publication Data
Names: Tsushima, Yūko, author. | Harcourt, Geraldine, translator.
Title: Territory of light / Yuko Tsushima ; translated from the Japanese by
    Geraldine Harcourt.
Other titles: Hikari no ryōbun. English
Description: First American edition. | New York : Farrar, Straus and Giroux,
    2019. | "Originally published in Japan in 1979 by Kodansha Ltd., Japan, as
    Hikari no Ryōbun. English translation rights arranged with the Estate of
    Yuko Tsushima through Japan UNI Agency, Inc., Tokyo. English translation
    originally published in 2018 by Penguin Books Ltd., Great Britain."
Identifiers: LCCN 2018033288 | ISBN 9780374273217 (hardcover)
Subjects: LCSH: Short stories, Japanese—Translations into English.
Classification: LCC PL862.S76 H513 2019 | DDC 895.63/5—dc23
LC record available at https://lccn.loc.gov/2018033288

Our books may be purchased in bulk for promotional, educational, or
business use. Please contact your local bookseller or the Macmillan
Corporate and Premium Sales Department at 1-800-221-7945, extension
5442, or by e-mail at MacmillanSpecialMarkets@macmillan.com.

www.fsgbooks.com
www.twitter.com/fsgbooks • www.facebook.com/fsgbooks

10 9 8 7 6 5 4 3 2 1

CONTENTS

TERRITORY OF LIGHT

The apartment had windows on all sides.

I spent a year there, with my little daughter, on the top floor of an old four-storey office building. We had the whole fourth floor to ourselves, plus the rooftop terrace. At street level there was a camera store; the second and third floors were both divided into two rented offices. A couple whose small business made custom gold family crests, framed or turned into trophy shields, occupied half a floor, as did an accountant and a branch of a knitting school, but the rooms on the third floor facing the main street happened to remain vacant all the time I lived above them. I used to slip in there some nights after my daughter had finally gone to sleep. I would open the windows a fraction and enjoy a different take on the view, or walk back and forth in the empty space. I felt as if I were in a secret chamber, unknown to anyone.

I was told that until I rented the fourth-floor apartment, the building's previous owner had lived there, and while this certainly had its perks – sole access to the rooftop and the spacious bathroom that had been built up there – it also meant that by default I was left in charge of the rooftop water tower and TV antenna, and that I had to go down late at night and lower the rolling security shutter at the stairwell entrance after the office tenants had all gone home, a task which naturally had been the owner's.

The whole building had gone up for sale and been bought by a locally famous businesswoman by the name of Fujino. I was to become the first resident of the newly christened Fujino Building No. 3. The owner herself was apparently new to the residential end of things, having specialized in commercial property till now, and, unsure about an apartment with an unusual layout in a dilapidated office building, she had tentatively proposed a low rent to see if there would be any takers. This happenstance was a lucky break for me. Also quite by chance, the man who at the time was still my husband had the same name as the building. As a result, I was constantly being mistaken for the proprietor.

At the top of the steep, narrow, straight stairs there was an aluminium door and, opposite that, a door to the fire escape. The landing was so small that you had to take a step down the stairs or up onto the threshold of the fire exit before being able to open the apartment door. The fire escape was actually an iron ladder, perpendicular to the ground. In an emergency, it looked like we might stand a better chance if I bolted down the main stairs with my daughter in my arms.

But once you got the door open, the apartment was filled with light at any hour of the day. The kitchen and dining area immediately inside had a red floor, which made the aura all the brighter. Entering from the dimness of the stairwell, you practically had to squint.

'Ooh, it's warm! It's pretty!' My daughter, who was about to turn three, gave a shout the first time she was bathed in the room's light.

'Isn't it cosy? The sun's great, isn't it?'

She ran around the dining-kitchen as she answered with a touch of pride, 'Yes! Didn't you know that, Mommy?'

I felt like giving myself a pat on the head for having managed to protect my daughter from the upheaval around her with the quantity of light.

The one window that caught the morning sun was in a cubbyhole beside the entrance, a kind of storage room less than two tatami mats in area. I decided to make that our bedroom. Its east-facing window overlooked platforms hung with laundry on top of the crowded neighbouring houses, and the roofs of office buildings smaller than Fujino No. 3. Because we were in a shopping district around a station on the main loop line, not one of the houses had a garden; instead, the neighbours lined up on the platforms and rooftops all the potted plants they could lay their hands on and even set out deckchairs, so that the view from above had a very homey feeling, and I often saw elderly people out there in their bathrobe *yukata*.

There were south-facing windows in every one of the straight line of rooms – the two-mat, the dining-kitchen, and the six-mat. These looked over the roof of an old low house and onto a lane of bars and eateries. For a narrow lane it saw a lot of traffic, with horns constantly blaring.

To the west, at the far end of the long, thin apartment, a big window gave onto the main road; here the late sun and the street noise poured in without mercy. Directly below, one could see the black heads of pedestrians who streamed along the pavement towards the station in the morning and back again in the evening. On the sidewalk opposite, in front of a florist's, people stood still at a bus stop. Every time a bus or truck passed by the whole fourth floor shook and the crockery rattled on the shelves. The building where I'd set up house with my daughter was on a three-way intersection – four-way counting the lane to the south. Nevertheless, several times a day, a certain conjunction of red lights and traffic flow would produce about ten seconds' silence. I always noticed it a split second before the signals changed and the waiting cars all revved impatiently at once.

To the left of this western window were just visible the trees of a wood that belonged to a large traditional garden, the site of a former daimyo's manor. That glimpse of greenery was precious to me. It was the centrepiece of the view from the window.

'That? Why, that's the Bois de Boulogne,' I answered whenever a visitor asked. The name of the wood on the outskirts of Paris had stuck in my mind, like Bremen or Flanders, some place named in a fairy tale, and it was kind of fun just to let it trip off my tongue.

Along the northern wall of the dining-kitchen were a closet, the toilet, and the stairs to the roof. The toilet had its own window, with a view of the station and the trains. That little window was my daughter's favourite.

'We can see the station and the trains! And the house shakes!' she proudly reported to her daycare teacher and friends at the start. But she quickly came down with a fever brought on by the move and spent nearly a week in bed. While I was at work I left her with my mother, who lived alone not far away. My job, at a library attached to a radio station, was to archive broadcast-related documents and tapes, and issue them on loan. At the end of the day I stopped by my mother's and stayed with my daughter till past nine, then returned alone to the building. My husband would no doubt have helped out if I'd contacted him, but I didn't want to rely on my husband, even if it meant putting my mother through extra trouble. In fact, I didn't want him ever to set foot in my new life. I was afraid of any renewed contact, so afraid it left me surprised at myself. The frightening thing was how accustomed I had become to his being there.

Before he left, he had been urging me to move back to my mother's. 'She must be lonesome, and besides, how are you going to manage with the little one on your own? With you two at your mom's, I could leave you without worrying.'

He had already chosen an apartment for himself along a suburban commuter line. He was due to move there in a month, when the place became vacant.

As for me, at that time I hadn't been able to get as far as thinking about where to go. His decision had yet to fully sink in. Wasn't there still a chance I'd hear him laugh it all off as a joke tomorrow? Then why should I worry about where I was going to live?

I told him I didn't want to go back to my mother's. 'Anything but that. That would just be trying to disguise the fact that you've left us.'

He then offered to come with me to look for an apartment. 'If you go by yourself you'll just get ripped off. I won't be able to sleep at night knowing you're in some dump. Come on, now, leave it to me.'

It was late January, and every day was bright and clear. I began doing the rounds of real estate agents with my husband. All I had to do was tag along without a word. I would meet him in my lunch hour at a café near my work and we'd go to the local agencies, one after the other.

He specified a 2DK (two rooms plus dining-kitchen), sunny, with bath, for around thirty thousand to forty thousand yen a month. The first place we tried, he was laughed at: 'These days you won't find anything like that for under sixty to seventy thousand.'

'It's actually for her and our child,' he said, looking back at me. 'Any old thing would do for me, but I want them to have the best possible . . . Are you sure you don't have something?'

The next day, exactly the same conversation took place at

another agency. Unable to contain myself, I whispered, 'The bath doesn't matter, really. And I'd be happy with one room.' Then I spoke up to the realtor: 'There are studios at thirty to forty thousand, aren't there?'

'Studios, yes . . .' He reached to open a ledger.

At this point my husband said sternly, as if scolding a child, 'You're too quick to give up. You're going about it the wrong way. Once you've settled in you'll find you can afford the rent, even if it seems a stretch right now. But you can't fix up a cheap apartment with the cash you save, the landlords don't allow alterations . . . So, what have you got in the fifty-to-sixty-thousand range?'

The realtor assured us that he could show us several possibilities in the fifty-thousand or, better still, the sixty-thousand-yen range. 'We'd like to see them,' said my husband. Considering he was so hard up he'd had to borrow from me to pay for the lease and security deposit on his own apartment, I could hardly expect him to provide financial support after the separation. He had been insisting that living apart was the only way out of the impasse in which he found himself – a clean sweep, a fresh start on his own. In that case, I wanted to pay my own way too and not cadge any more from my mother. The maximum rent I could afford was therefore fifty thousand yen, which was what the place where we'd been living together cost. I calculated that without my husband's living expenses to cover, I should be able to get by without borrowing. But it was a calculation made with gritted teeth. Fifty thousand yen was more than half my monthly pay.

That day, we were shown a sixty-thousand-yen rental condominium. There was nothing not to like and it was handy for the office, but I didn't take it.

Almost every day, we toured a variety of vacancies. We looked at a seventy-thousand-yen condominium with a garden. And a policy of no children. My husband appealed to the landlord that it was just the one child, a girl, and she'd be away all day at daycare, but I could have told him it would do no good.

The viewings were creeping steadily upmarket. I was now able to shrug off hearing a rent that amounted to my entire pay. I felt neither uneasy nor conscious of the absurdity. We were enthusiastically inspecting apartments I couldn't possibly rent, and we were apparently dead serious. But neither my husband nor I saw ourselves as the one doing the renting. He was accompanying me, and I was accompanying him.

'Are we going again today?'

This question had become part of our morning routine. Weather permitting, most of my lunch hours were taken up by a busy whirl. And from January into early February every day was as fine as could be.

There was a house with a Japanese cypress beside its front entrance. At the top of five stone steps, a light-blue door beckoned. The door was barely three feet from the steps; the tree had just enough room to grow. Its branches hid a bay window whose frame had been painted the same colour as the front door.

'This is quite something.' My husband sounded excited.

'But I don't care for that tree. I'd rather have a magnolia, say, or a cherry . . .'

'A cypress has way more class.'

It was a two-storey house. Downstairs were a room with a wooden floor and bay windows, a six-tatami room that didn't get much light, and a dining-kitchen; upstairs were two well-lit tatami rooms and even a place to hang out laundry. By the time we checked out the laundry deck, both my husband and I were very nearly euphoric. Aware of the agent within earshot, we said to each other, all smiles:

'I bet your friends would be happy to come over.'

'And there's plenty of room for them to stay . . .'

'It'd be a great place to bring up a child. Easy for me to drop in too . . . I'm starting to envy you, I'd like to rent it myself. I'd have my desk by that window . . .'

'The bookshelves can go along that wall.'

'Right . . . Hey, I know, let me be your lodger. I'll pay room and board on the dot.'

'Sure. But you're not getting a discount.'

As our laughter echoed in the empty rooms, it brought a weak smile to the realtor's lips.

I couldn't help thinking, once again, that I was never going to have to live alone with our daughter. If I could live with my husband I didn't care where, and without him everywhere was equally daunting.

Back at the library that day, for a while I pictured life in the two-storey house. My husband had enthused, 'Take it, don't worry about the rent, just get your family to help you,' and then disappeared. I would put the stereo in the room with the bay windows and use that space for meals and for relaxing. I'd make the dark six-mat room downstairs our bedroom and keep the upstairs for guests until my daughter was older. No, on second thought, the sunny, spacious upper floor was obviously more comfortable. I wondered who would visit, apart from my husband. Since it was close to the office, would my colleagues come if I invited them?

As I was immersed in these thoughts, a high school teacher from out of town asked to borrow some tapes of poetry readings for classroom use. My mind still far away, I inserted the series one by one in a tape recorder. We always had borrowers listen to a part of the tapes we issued to ensure they were the right ones.

For some reason, the words on the tape suddenly registered with me.

> Quick now, give up this idle pondering!
> And let's be off into the great wide world!
> I tell you: the fool who speculates on things
> is like some animal on a dry heath,

led by an evil fiend in endless circles,

while fine green pastures lie on every side.

Startled, I asked the teacher standing there, 'What was that?' Could that be poetry, I was wondering. He glanced at the window, evidently thinking I'd heard something outside, then cocked his head to one side with a puzzled smile.

My husband didn't come home that night, nor the next. He was probably convinced that my new location had been decided.

I began to go around the agencies by myself. It was the first time I'd entered a realtor's all alone.

The voice on the tape had reminded me of my last move, four years ago. The memory had caught me by surprise.

My husband was still a grad student and I hadn't been working long at the library. Though we each had our own apartment, half the time he spent the night at mine. I had a call from him one day at the library: 'We have an apartment. It's new, and quiet, and sunny. It's fantastic. I said we'd move in on Sunday. OK?'

It had been only the night before that we'd raised the subject of needing to look for a place for the two of us.

'That was fast. You said we'd take it?' Though astonished, I was also delighted by the effortlessness of the decision. I was not annoyed at having had no say in where I was to live.

I was enjoying the feeling of being swept along by a man. I'd left home to be free to have him stay over and he'd found the place for me that time too, a room in a student boarding-house used by his friends. But it had taken him a while to make up his mind that I was the one.

All I had to do was follow his instructions. I packed on Saturday night and was ready in the morning when the truck came around after stopping at his apartment. I had so little to load, it was the work of a moment. I joined him riding in the back and we set off, me with a stack of LPs on my lap, him with a shopping bag full of laundry in his arms.

In about thirty minutes we arrived. The new place was down a cul-de-sac in a residential area.

'Is this it?' I exclaimed happily. It was my first sight of my own apartment.

We lived there for a year and a half, until I became pregnant.

Which meant I had never even found myself a place to live before now, I realized. Bizarre though it seemed, I had to admit it was true.

I made the rounds on my own, meticulously, in the vicinity of my daughter's daycare. Before I knew it we were into March. Inevitably, the low-rent properties I was asking to see were a far cry from those I'd toured with my husband, and I often felt like retreating in dismay. However, the more of those gloomy, cramped apartments I looked at, the further the figure of my husband receded from sight, and while the rooms were invariably dark, I began to sense a gleam in their darkness like that of an animal's eyes. There was something there glaring back at me. Although it scared me, I wanted to approach it.

Once, offered a real bargain, a very nice 2DK unit in a condominium building for thirty thousand yen, I went dubiously to look at it. Everything about it was normal, as far as I could see.

'But this doesn't make sense. Why is it so cheap?'

The realtor reluctantly confessed the truth, since I was bound to find out anyhow. 'There was a family suicide. Gas, so it's not as if it left traces. It was said to be a murder-suicide after a divorce battle. It was in the papers. And as if that weren't bad enough, when a couple moved in next, the wife went and hanged herself . . . Yes, hanged herself. It beats me, it really does. The place has been empty ever since. It's been a year now.'

'I see . . . Then it was a sort of chain reaction? She must have thought she could stay untouched by the deaths,' I said, fighting down an urgent desire to get out of there.

'I expect you're right. They've changed the tatami and repainted the walls, but of course the gas valve is still in the same position. That's it there.'

The realtor pointed to a corner of the smaller room. A heap of corpses met my eyes on the tatami, toppled around the outlet.

'She couldn't help seeing the bodies, I guess . . .'

'She seems to have had a breakdown. She'd only just arrived from her hometown . . .'

I said I'd think about it and made my escape. 'There's no hurry, it won't be snapped up,' the agent counselled. But though I wasn't superstitious, I wasn't sure I could stay unaffected, either.

A few evenings later, a different realtor escorted me to a tall, thin building. From below my first reaction had been a sigh at the sight of the formidable stairs, but the minute he opened the place up and I took one step inside, I crowed to myself that this was the apartment for me. The red floor blazed in the setting sun. The long-closed, empty rooms pulsed with light.

The first cherry blossoms were coming out by the time my daughter, made ill by exhaustion after the move, was well enough to start back at daycare. I taught her 'Sakura, Sakura' along with 'The Little Bleating Goat' and the song about the crow. Our voices boomed inside the bathroom, but it felt even better to belt the songs out on the rooftop. I was impressed, I admit, to discover I had such a fine voice. I bought a supply of nursery rhyme books and sang my way through them between bursts of applause from my daughter. In the back of my mind I was listening to the words I'd heard on the tape: *Give up this idle pondering.*

In tears of excitement, my daughter showered me with 'Encores' and 'Bravos' she'd picked up from a picture book.

I didn't know my husband's new address. All I'd been given was the phone number of the restaurant where he was now working part-time. Someone had told me that his new woman friend was the owner, and that she was old enough to be his mother. She might be just what he needed, I thought, after he'd led a group of his friends in trying to start a small theatre company and ended with nothing to show for it but debts.

He hadn't been pleased at my deciding on a new place by myself, and had moved out before me, still aggrieved. I no longer had any intention of letting him into my apartment.

He would come, though. While afraid of that moment, at the same time I was beginning to be aware that I couldn't turn his way once again. And this after I'd been so unwilling to break up in the first place. I was puzzled by how I had changed. But I could no longer go back.

Quick now, give up this idle pondering. And let's be off!

So I told myself. My daughter had yet to notice her father's disappearance.

'. . . In the summer, let's have a paddling pool on the roof. There's room for a big one,' I said as I put her to bed. 'And let's have a couple of sun-loungers as well. I could go for a beer too. Shall we string up fairy lights like the rooftop beer gardens do? Won't they be pretty? And let's plant lots of flowers. Sunflowers and dahlias and cannas. Shall we keep a rabbit? A guinea pig would be nice. But actually we could keep an even bigger animal. A goat – why not? And how about chickens? That's it, we'll have a farm. Won't the neighbours be surprised when the cow goes moo . . .'

My daughter was watching my mouth with wide eyes. I stroked her head.

The two-mat bedroom was as small as a closet, and I felt at home.

THE WATER'S EDGE

During the night, there had been a sound of water on the other side of the wall. In my sleep I was looking out from the fourth-floor bedroom at nearby buildings bathed in rain, gleaming with neon and streetlamp colours. It was a light, tenuous sound. I couldn't say at what hour of the night it had started. It could well have been there when I went to bed; then again, it could have been an illusion as I was on the brink of waking.

In the morning, when I opened the windows wide, dazzling sunlight burst in, together with the thrum of traffic. The sky was pure blue. The streets were dry. Perfectly dry, even in the shade.

Happy to see another fine day, I set about waking my daughter without wondering where the night's rain could have got to, leaving not the slightest puddle. I had a feeling that it was still raining elsewhere, someplace like that spot I couldn't quite reach behind my back. It was a lingering sensation, close at hand, of water in the distance. I had almost dismissed it as a dream, but not entirely.

If the downstairs tenant hadn't kicked up a fuss, I would no doubt have listened to the same splashing again that night, harboured the same not-unpleasant sensation the next morning, and then forgotten all about it.

Just as I bit into a slice of toast, I heard a knock at the door. Who on earth could that be so early in the morning? More warily than necessary, I opened the door. A vaguely familiar face appeared, a portly man in late middle age. I couldn't place him at first. It was a bit of a letdown that it wasn't Fujino, whom I hadn't seen since our separation, over a month ago.

'The water – are you having some kind of problem up here?' the man asked, scanning the room irritably. My daughter stood in front of him and curiously observed us in turn, her head tilted back. 'The water! You've spilled some, or let the bath overflow, haven't you? You'd better do something quick. We've got a real mess on our hands.'

It finally dawned on me that this was the man from the office on the floor below. After hurriedly greeting him properly, I replied, 'How do you mean? Everything's all right here.'

'I'm telling you, there's a flood downstairs. The leak has to be coming from your place. If you haven't noticed it yet, go and have a look around now, please.'

He was the owner of the company that made gold-plated trophy shields. They probably didn't actually produce them in the small office downstairs, but there were always cartons stacked, ready for shipping, in the open doorway. I had seen this man several times, hefting boxes or checking the contents against a ledger. Whether overloaded with work or just a born hard worker, he arrived around eight every morning and then often stayed till near midnight. His presence was rather a nuisance to me, since it was my job, as the only resident in a building occupied by offices, to raise and lower the shutter at the street entrance. It can't have been too convenient for him either to be kept waiting in front of the closed shutter whenever I overslept, or to have to give me a call through the door last thing at night. It had been a month since the company moved in, and after another month of this the landlady would give him his own key to the shutter, a special favour that came as a relief to me too.

The man's wife, who was his only employee, was generally obliged to work late with him. But I had never really gotten a good look at her face. While he was regularly to be seen bustling in the doorway with the boxes, she invariably kept her head down at the desk in the room behind. In her apron, she seemed dressed for scouring pots in the kitchen.

Since the man insisted the leak must be somewhere on the fourth floor, I made a tour of the plumbing just in case, checking the kitchen faucets, washing machine, toilet, and the rooftop bathroom that opened off the inside stairs, conscious all along of the fast-approaching hour at which I had to leave for work. I checked the six-tatami room while I was at it. As I expected, there was not a drop of water.

'It doesn't seem to be coming from here,' I reported. In the excitement of this unusual morning, my daughter hadn't touched her breakfast. 'Hurry up and drink your milk,' I scolded. 'We're leaving in a minute. You'll get into trouble with your teacher again.'

'Look, lady, don't give me that. What's this puddle doing here, then? Here. Come on, you won't see it from in there.'

The man backed down two steps in the narrow stairwell and glowered at me, so there was nothing for it: I stepped outside in my slippers. He slammed the door and pointed at the landing. He was right, there was actually a small puddle on the floor. I looked up at the ceiling. That could have been a water stain in the corner, but the ceiling in my apartment had similar marks. The realtor had explained those away: the rain had leaked in badly at one time, but the terraced rooftop had since been completely repaired.

'. . . Well, I don't know, surely this puddle can't be –' As I spoke, my daughter burst into tears on the other side of the door. I reached to open it, and the man grabbed my arm.

'The water is obviously coming from this floor,' he said. 'I've left my wife to cope, and she doesn't know which way to turn. Because when we opened up, we found all our files soaking wet. Come down and have a look. You'll see.'

My daughter was crying harder. Brushing the man aside, I tried to wrestle the door open. With nowhere to stand on the tiny landing, he scrambled out of the way down the steps.

After scooping up my howling daughter, who was hot all over, I told him, 'In any case, we've established the leak isn't in here. Would you mind checking again on your side? I have to go to work now, so please come back this evening if there's still a problem. I'll be home at six.'

And without waiting for his answer I shut the door. He went downstairs without further protest. It was already time to get going. As my daughter clung to my shoulder, I wiped her flushed face with a wet cloth, then gave up on breakfast and rushed out. I crept down the stairs, afraid of being hailed again. Through the office's open door, I could hear the man venting his frustration by swearing at his wife.

The leak he had reported concerned me very little. My daughter had gone without breakfast, and instead of waving her usual cheerful goodbye at the daycare centre, she pressed herself against me and let out a wail, trembling as though the teachers would devour her if she took a step in their direction. Two of them were eventually needed to march her indoors and I ended up late for work, on top of everything. As a result, I was less worried about the water than annoyed at having the start of my day disrupted for no good reason. What made him think he had the right to come to a stranger's door and carry on like that? The man's behaviour seemed the height of self-ishness, and I held it against him. I had completely forgotten the faint splashing I had heard in the night.

During the lunch break Fujino called as I was having my sandwich and carton of milk at my desk, as usual, across from Kobayashi, my immediate boss at the music library. 'It's your husband,' Kobayashi said, and passed the receiver offhandedly. Murmuring 'Thanks,' I put it to my ear. I heard Fujino's familiar voice. The awareness that I'd missed that voice instantly gave way to a rush of fury. I could not even manage to speak in a natural, normal tone, despite all my promises to myself that if Fujino got in touch we would catch up casually, if only so as not to complicate the way things were between us, with our daughter in the middle, and that one day I would try to find the words to explain why, in the end, it was me who'd decided I wanted to split up – though, admittedly, I didn't understand too well myself how I'd arrived there.

I was acutely conscious of Kobayashi listening. There had been another call from Fujino that he had passed over to me, four years earlier. We were living together at the time but not yet officially married. I don't remember what the call was about; perhaps we discussed meeting somewhere for dinner. As Fujino was receiving both a scholarship from his university and an allowance from his parents, we were better off financially in those days than at any other time in our four years together, and we often ate out. I was content with my new life, which didn't require much in the way of domesticity. And, as usual, I had chatted that day without particularly caring that Kobayashi was within earshot.

When I replaced the receiver, however, he had looked up and said, 'I hope everything works out for you soon.'

I blushed, startled: I had thought of him as an old man too absorbed in his archives and his books to have any interest in his assistant's private life. Had he been listening to all our phone calls, then? I hadn't told him that I had started living with Fujino, but he must have been taking it all in. In fact, why wouldn't he, when I came to think about it, but my boss's tactfulness had escaped my attention till then.

'It gets tiring when you take forever to settle down, especially for the woman . . . Take good care of yourself.'

I nodded, disconcerted.

Kobayashi had been a radio presenter. An unlikely one, I thought, with his hoarse voice, but in any event, nearly twenty years into his career, there'd apparently been some personal trouble that led to his being transferred from one section to another until he ended up in charge of the library that was being set up in an annex. He was a gruff man in his sixties who always looked unwell, but his young colleagues had given him quite an affectionate nickname, 'Chairman of the Board.' A good many of them would stop by to pass the time. They seemed to say things expressly to provoke him, as if it amused them to watch the changes in his dour expression. I gathered also, from these exchanges, that he lived as a bachelor.

After Kobayashi spoke up, I'd felt both oddly touched by his concern and damned if I was going to let him feel sorry for me, which, together, made me smile more often in his direction. Kobayashi, for his part, took to inviting me out for a coffee during office hours, or for a drink after work in a bar where he was a regular with his name on a bottle of whisky. 'Help yourself anytime,' he urged me. 'A woman's entitled to have a drink when she feels like it too.' But I could hardly drink his whisky with Fujino, and I never called in at the bar unless I was in Kobayashi's company. As there wasn't really anything for the two of us to have deep discussions about, I found his kindness a little burdensome. Kobayashi remained dour wherever he was and however much he drank; he talked about work and books, and never referred to my private life again. After walking me to the station, it seemed he would head for another bar in a different area. His fondness for alcohol was known to everyone at work.

All the same, though he refrained from giving me advice, I had perhaps sensed from this new sociability of his that he was a little worried about me, and when Fujino and I got formally married, the first person I wanted to announce it to was not my mother but Kobayashi. While it was true that I sometimes resented Kobayashi and even wondered what he was playing at when, as always, I was called to account by Fujino on getting home late after these evenings – 'You just don't care that you live with me, do you?' he'd say, among other accusations – at the same time, I felt sure that Kobayashi would be more pleased than anyone to hear the news of our marriage.

When I made the announcement, adding apologetically that I knew I'd caused him to worry, Kobayashi gave a wry smile and muttered, 'It's nothing to do with me.' That was his only comment. But I felt as though I had received his good wishes, and dipped my head again, smiling.

I no longer went to the bar with Kobayashi after that – for one thing, I was soon pregnant. Instead, as it happened, we got into the habit of spending a leisurely lunchtime together at our facing desks, after I'd gone out for sandwiches, buying his along with my own. We often listened to music on a little radio I'd brought, or sampled Kobayashi's favourites among the archived programmes, and sometimes a visitor would join us, lunchbox in hand; once the baby arrived, I would often hold forth all lunch hour, explaining to Kobayashi how cute and funny she was, even showing him photos. I also regaled him with a lecture on the 'new cinema,' which Fujino had stayed on at university to study and to which he wanted to dedicate his life. On that occasion too, after hearing me out he'd had just one thing to say: 'Kids grow up so fast – think of all the home movies he could be making.'

Thus, knowing Kobayashi, I knew he could not have failed to notice that, over the last year or so, I had gradually grown more reserved. And once I started giving up my lunch breaks to make the rounds of realtors, it must have been increasingly obvious how my life had changed. But even when I informed him of my new address, I couldn't bring myself to say anything about the situation with Fujino. I cringed at the reminder of how thoroughly I'd once congratulated myself.

As I took the receiver, then, I cursed Fujino: Why the hell did he have to phone me here? What did he expect me to say, with Kobayashi listening? I'd been persuading myself that, from now on, we would talk things over calmly, and if, by any chance, this meant we could live together again, that would be best. But now, caught unprepared, I tensed, determined to blame it all on Fujino: This wasn't the time and place. It would wreck everything. Look what you've gone and done.

'It's been a while,' he said. 'How are you, how's our little girl, how are you finding the new apartment, it's about time we got together, come on, say something, ah, there's someone there, isn't there, well, OK, but still, you could say *something*, it's your husband calling, what's wrong with being heard? Hello, are you there? You could at least say *yes*. Is that too much to ask?'

After letting him run out of words, I said tightly, 'Why are you calling?'

'Huh! So I'm not allowed to phone you unless it's on business?'

'No . . . Goodbye . . .'

I hung up. Unable to face Kobayashi, I munched on my sandwich with eyes downcast. When I finally glanced up at him, over the milk I was drinking, he was buried in the newspaper, hamburger in hand. Fujino didn't call back, perhaps not wanting to pursue this at my workplace. But knowing how angry he must be, I was aghast at what I'd done and couldn't help regretting it. My legs shook, the back of my throat ached. It was me, not Fujino, who had wrecked everything. It was surely hopeless now.

As I stood up, twisting the empty milk carton and paper bag in both hands, Kobayashi said, 'Could you get me a cup of tea, if you wouldn't mind? I've got a thirst today.'

I lifted my head at last and answered with the brightest 'Yes' I could manage.

I went into the kitchenette behind a partition and made two cups of green tea with care. My legs were still shaky. I was just about at Kobayashi's desk when I teetered, though there was nothing to trip me, and both cups were sent flying off the tray. Mine didn't break when it hit the floor; Kobayashi's large cup did.

Murmuring 'Oh dear, I'm sorry . . . I'm sorry,' I crouched and picked up the pieces. The cup had split almost cleanly in two. I heard Kobayashi's voice above my head.

'You'll cut yourself if you're not careful. You should mop it up with a cloth.'

'Oh, yes, sorry. I'll, er, I'll be right back.'

I ran half-stooping to the kitchenette, not taking the time to straighten up. I grabbed a cloth, returned to the spot in front of Kobayashi, kneeled, and pressed the cloth to the steaming floor. The liquid's heat reached my palm at once.

'Your cup is tougher than it looks, isn't it?'

When I raised my head, Kobayashi was comparing my cup, which he had in his hand, with the pieces of his own lying on the desk, where I must have tossed them a moment earlier.

'. . . I'm sorry.'

'Don't worry. It was only a free giveaway at a sushi bar, anyway.'

'Yes . . .'

The heat in the cloth was rapidly dissipating. I suddenly remembered that morning's events and asked Kobayashi, 'Er . . . Could a little spill like this leak through to the floor below?'

'I'd be very surprised. If this much could leak through, no one could live in a high-rise,' he answered, to my relief, giving a rare laugh.

'Yes, of course.' I laughed in turn and stared at the still-damp linoleum. I slid the cloth over it. Tears sprang to my eyes. I wiped them surreptitiously with my left hand as I kept mopping up, taking my time.

Before long, Kobayashi went to the toilet. While he was gone, I cleared the cloth and the broken china away, then started preparing new loan cards. The lunch hour was already over.

At the end of the afternoon, a little earlier than usual, Kobayashi told me I could go, that we'd finished for the day. I took off without a moment's hesitation. My daughter leaped with joy when her mother showed up before the appointed time, and we did some shopping on the way back to the apartment. We had barely set foot on the stairs when the man I'd seen that morning emerged from his third-floor office, my daughter's shrill voice having no doubt announced our presence. The realtor who managed the building was visible behind him. It was not hard to guess from their expressions how impatiently they'd been awaiting my return. Barely restraining the desire to turn on my heel and flee the building, I climbed slowly, one step at a time, letting my daughter go ahead. She clambered up the steep stairs on all fours, like a dog.

When we reached the third-floor landing, the realtor stepped forward as if to shield his glowering companion with his own slight frame. 'I'm sorry to bother you. Actually, we've been waiting over an hour. This gentleman wanted me to unlock the upstairs apartment, but I suggested it would be better to wait, as you were sure to be home anytime now, and I took the liberty of waiting with him . . .'

'Wait, he says,' the man fumed. 'There's not a moment to lose.'

The realtor smiled reassuringly at me. 'There does seem to be a serious leak. There's water dripping down to the second storey now, and since it isn't raining, I'd have to say it's coming from the top floor. I'm very sorry to inconvenience you, but would you allow me to make a quick check?'

The realtor was a thin, white-haired man. The sixtyish businesswoman who owned the building had been sitting on his office sofa when I went to pay the rent, and together they had something of the air of a chatelaine and her elderly butler. He was a quiet, rather distinguished old man.

I led the way upstairs. What had been a small puddle that morning was now wetting the whole of the fourth-floor landing. The stain on the ceiling had spread as well. A droplet grew there lazily, reached a certain size, then fell, and the process started over.

I first asked the two men to wait in the entrance while I took a look around inside. Nothing had changed since the morning. In the intense late-afternoon sun, the interior was dazzlingly bright, shimmering around me as if the rooms held a heat haze. My daughter never left my side, singing at the top of her voice a song she'd just learned at daycare.

I finished by sticking my head into the bedroom. Confident there was no problem there, I did so merely to rest my case with the man downstairs, but for the first time I discovered traces of water on one of the walls. Where the previous day I hadn't noticed anything, a large stain had appeared. On the other side of that wall was the stairwell.

I reported the discovery. The man was raring to go in. 'No, excuse me, would you mind not going in there? Let's have a look on the roof. I didn't check the terrace this morning.'

I led them hastily to the inside stairs. The thought of anyone seeing my unmade futon left out on the tatami made me tense.

There was nothing out of place in the bathroom. I opened

the door that led onto the rooftop and was the first to cross the threshold. I let out a cry of astonishment at the sight that met my eyes. Where there should have been a perfectly dry roof, water rippled and sparkled. A great expanse of clear water.

'The sea! Mommy, it's the sea! Wow! Look how big it is!'

My daughter plunged in, barefoot. Laughing to herself in merry peals, she paddled, splashed with her feet, scooped with her hands, dipped her face. On her, the pool was ankle deep.

The three of us traced the flow to the building's water tower. Water was spurting from it in a mesmerizing jet.

'It arrives at the drain over there, and the overflow has been seeping downstairs,' said the realtor. 'It must be getting through a little crack somewhere. But . . . what a view.'

The man from the third floor, also awed, perhaps, had completely regained his composure. 'Well, well, we can count ourselves lucky to have gotten off so lightly downstairs.'

'Look, your little girl is having the time of her life.'

'My grandchildren love to paddle too.'

The two men gazed at my daughter frolicking, their eyes lighting up with pleasure.

'But you were directly underneath, surely you heard something?' At the realtor's remark I remembered, for the first time, the sound of water in the night. That gentle, distant sound. A sound that would be revisiting me in my waking hours: I felt a chill, as if I'd been caught off guard.

'Now that you mention it, I did hear something . . . But then, this morning, when I saw the sky so clear . . . somehow I didn't . . .'

'Oh, really?' said the man from the third floor. 'If you'd only dealt with it then, we could have had it repaired right away.' I bowed my head and apologized lamely.

Having agreed that the repairmen would come first thing the next day, the two went on their way.

That night, I took off my shoes and had a high old time in the rooftop 'sea' with my daughter. Though there was no way it could be dangerous, it was a little unnerving to venture into the expanse of water, and the uneasiness gave me a thrill. We splashed each other and played tag till we ended up soaked. The air was chilly on wet skin. However warm the days might be, it was still only the beginning of May.

Just as we returned indoors the phone stopped ringing, having rung, I imagine, for quite some time. Fujino's face came to mind. Along with it came the sound of my own voice, asking Kobayashi if I would always have to answer for having happily set up house with Fujino, for having gone so joyfully to the registry office, for having had a child with him so unhesitatingly. Kobayashi seemed to be nodding yes. All at once, countless shadowy figures loomed around me, agreeing vigorously.

This man was my daughter's father and my husband, but he knew nothing of the life I had been leading for over a month now – an existence that was uneventful enough in its way, and yet the tranquillity of the days ahead only fed my apprehension – and I could give him no idea of that life. I felt as though I had before me an invisible, rickety, misshapen mass that not only kept its precarious balance but was actually sending out roots and even tentative new shoots that only my eyes could see. Having been presented with this unstable object, I was starting to grow too attached to it to be able to slip back into married life with Fujino as if nothing had happened. The way he spoke to me, as my husband, didn't feel right anymore. Must I go on, still, listening to that distant and increasingly incomprehensible voice until he decided to break off ties?

Was I supposed never to forget Fujino, even though it was he who'd wanted the separation? Again I contemplated the shadowy figures, each of which reminded me of a person I knew. They nodded deeply, all together.

That night, too, the sound of water lapped about my ears. I slept nestled in a sense of moisture.

The next morning, the repair work was over in no time. The rooftop was emptied of its transparent water before our eyes. My daughter spoke for me when she told the repairmen indignantly, 'Don't stop the water! Meanies! I hate you!'

Two days later, a Sunday, the roof was mended, a job that took all day. In the evening, on learning the work was finished, I went up for a look. We'd been warned to keep off the surface until it was completely dry, as I reminded my daughter repeatedly on the way up the stairs.

When she opened the door and saw the rooftop, ahead of me, she let out an even more piercing squeal than when she'd discovered 'the sea,' and began to make a commotion.

Muttering, 'What's the matter?' I poked my head out. I couldn't believe what I saw: the whole surface was a bright, shining silver. Its dazzling sheen hurt the back of my eyes. I'd thought they were just going to fill the cracks, but they had painted every inch of the roof with waterproof paint. If it was this bright in the spring, by summer it would be unbearable. The glare would burn our eyes, here in the midst of the city, as if we were crossing a snowfield or adrift at sea.

A silver sea.

I couldn't help laughing. This too was a fine view, I told myself. And this time, nobody could take the sea away.

'It's beautiful, it's like a star.' My daughter gazed in admiration at the silvery roof.

It was the following night that Fujino called. The only things I could manage to say just aggravated his feelings. I couldn't understand why my legs shook every time I heard his voice.

That same night I dreamed I was sitting in a silver, star-shaped receptacle. It was spinning, gradually turning faster and faster, until I found my body plastered flat against its wall by centrifugal force. When I begged aloud for forgiveness, an old classmate from middle school looked up at my star and said: *Why are you such a loser?*

We'd been in the same class, certainly, but she was an A student, and we'd never been close. She was always elected class president and, what's more, she was good-looking and popular with the boys. While thinking how absurd it was to dream of her after all these years, I was defending myself tearfully: *Can I help it if I'm a loser? And even if I am, there are people who won't give up on me, who'll stick around. There are, there must be.*

The classmate shook her head sadly and walked away, still the same beautiful girl.

SUNDAY IN THE TREES

Three large trees met my eyes after we came through the main gate. They were zelkova elms so tall they stood out even in the 'Bois de Boulogne.' It was the first time I'd noticed them – or their height, rather – despite having been there often since I was a child. I stopped beneath them to gaze up into their tops. Raring to go on, my daughter pulled my arm with unexpected strength; I teetered repeatedly but held my ground.

We were just inside the entrance, which was flanked on the left by the office and the public toilets. The dank little toilet block, surrounded by dark shrubbery, had a pervasive odour that mingled with those of the earth and the trees. The only people lingering in such a spot either were kicking their heels outside the toilets waiting for their companions or were first-time visitors from far away taking a moment to study the information board with its guide map and history of the garden. Most of the crowd strode off along the gravel path marked with small white route indicators. My daughter was impatient to do the same.

'It's that way. Hurry up, we'll miss it. What are you look-ing at?'

'What'll we miss? Just look at the size of these trees.'

'Come *on*, it's that way! Everybody's going.'

'Just take a look, up there.'

'No-o-o!'

I had never noticed that there were such tall trees in front of the gate. Returning my gaze to the tops of the three elms, I wondered why I'd noticed them on that particular day. Their presence before my eyes now was the odd thing, odder than not having seen them before. Their crowns were them-selves tall. Slender and straight, they gave me an uneasy sense that I was about to be lifted off the ground and sucked into the soft, light-filled sky. The early-summer leaves were still young; they stirred coolly at the tips of the branches, giving off tiny gleams that flitted like insects.

'Mommy!'

'Don't do that, you'll pull my arm out of its socket.'

'I'll pull it to bits.'

'Ouch! That's enough, young lady.'

'Mommy, come *on*! Can't you hear me?'

'I can hear you . . .'

I still hadn't taken my eyes off the zelkovas. They were rooted at the points of a triangle, but their branches over-lapped, and the closer they got to the sky, the harder it became to tell which of them belonged to which trunk. I tried to trace the intricate mesh till my eyes swam and the whole began to resemble some plant species, expelled from the sky, which in a fit of disgruntlement had stiffened into these three brooding pillars as it landed.

'Walk! Stupidhead!'

More footsteps, a mixture of heavy and light, approached me from behind, skirted around me, and faded towards the gravel path. The impetuous steps of children. Mothers dragging their heels. People were streaming in at the gate almost without pause.

'Move this leg! Move it!' My daughter had her arms around my leg and was lifting it, so that I had to grab the trunk of the nearest elm to keep my balance.

'Hey! Let go of me. I said let go!'

'No-o! I'm going to smash up this leg.'

'Oh, yeah? You've bitten off more than you can chew, kid.'

As I spoke I swivelled this way and that with her astride my leg, then, as she still wouldn't let go, I peered down at her face. She glared back at me, pale with anger. There was no sign of childish tears or a conciliatory smile. Was she saying it was all my fault? The thought was barely formed before I had given her a swift slap on the cheek and was blurting, 'So, take off, then, if you're so keen. Go on! You're not the only one who's fed up, you know. There's a limit to what I can stand. You've been carrying on all day: *you're* lonely, *you're* bored – don't you ever stop to think about me? You made such a fuss about coming here, and now I've brought you. So go on, don't just stand there, get going.'

I gave her a shove on the forehead. She retreated one step at a time, her mouth open, aghast, and when she backed into someone walking past, her face crumpled and she turned away from me and dashed off. She was out of sight in no time.

Alone, I was suddenly conscious of the eyes of passersby and hastily glanced back up into the elm branches. I felt vertigo. I wasn't sure what I'd done. I was afraid of my child: that fear, which I could still feel inside me, was all I knew. Here was I, a mother trying to take her child's father from her. A mother who, for no good reason, was pulling her child over to her own side at the father's expense.

I heard his voice: 'So tell me, what makes you think you're a better parent than me?' I had no answer.

'Daddy's right, I like him much better. I wish you'd take me to Daddy's place.'

Why were children the only ones who ever got to melt down? This child whose father was Fujino. A father who was already living with another woman, and who in reality had no intention of taking custody of his child. A father who never once sent money. And yet, did the child I was raising belong to him, after all? Was this tiredness simply the parting gift I'd be left one day when I surrendered her, once she was grown, to Fujino? He was her father and that was that, no matter how much I yelled and screamed.

I wished I could forget I even had a child. I'd been coping on my own now for less than six months, though maybe that was just long enough to have grown used to the new life, which could be why the insidious tiredness was starting to knock the wind out of me. I had to admit to myself that when we were together, I'd depended on Fujino to hold me up. It only added to my fatigue that I was determined not to let him guess I felt this way.

I'd seen him several days earlier. He'd called and said, 'I'm in the coffee shop just down the street. Come on down, or I'm coming up.' And so I went, after getting our daughter off to sleep. And I managed to come right out and ask him to wait a while before seeing her, because she was doing well at present and it would be better to leave her be. What I was really thinking, deep down, was that with time she might forget her father and he might get over it. He wasn't taken in, however: after accusing me of selfishness, he couldn't leave without slapping my cheek, just as I'd now slapped hers, and hurling back over his shoulder, 'Give me a break! I'm going, but don't think for one second that you've heard the last of this.'

It may have been only natural for him to act that way, but on reaching home that night I'd shed tears, gripped by a longing that I knew was senseless: why, instead of slapping me, instead of shouting, couldn't he have taken me in his arms? At that moment the question of our child could wait. I had been weeping for the loss of the man I'd believed to be closer to me than anybody.

I heard a child's voice to my right. I looked around: it was

some child I didn't know, calling to his mother in front of
the toilets.

I broke into a run towards the gravel path. Could I catch
up? How far could she have gone? Maybe she was hiding
behind those shrubs, watching me. I peered into their shadows: there was no one there. I called my daughter's name as
I ran. There was no answer. The supposedly crowded park
was hushed. The path was very hard to run on in sandals. I
fumed at the gravel every time I stumbled: why'd they have
to use so much? The masses of trees annoyed me too.

The nickname 'Bois de Boulogne' was too good for this
gloomy Japanese garden, I thought, and at that moment I
remembered the large pond in its centre. In my mind's eye,
my daughter's body drifted gently on the surface. Was I
going to be taught a lesson for saying those things and slapping her? I tore off my apron and headed for the pond,
thrusting the air aside with both hands as if stroking through
shadowy blue depths.

That morning, as always on Sundays, it had been nearly
noon before I'd contemplated getting up. More than once I'd
woken at the sound of my daughter's voice, only to fall asleep
again. She'd gone back to sleep herself, perhaps tired of
shaking my sluggardly body, but when she next woke she set
about getting me out of bed once and for all. She snatched
the quilt, sat astraddle me, pulled my hair, and bombarded
me, hard, with her blocks and books. As I slept on regardless, she burst into tears: 'I'm hu-ungry.'

Every week, the morning of my one day off plays out the same way. 'There's milk, sliced bread, whatever you want, just help yourself,' I tell her, not opening my eyes. The lull that follows allows me to drop trustingly off again, until my daughter breaks into more tears: I spilled the milk. I wet my pants. The glass broke . . . Reluctantly I sit up, look at her, and survey the room. There is a pool of milk, glints of broken glass, a scattering of toys on the floor. The refrigerator door is open. Her finger is bleeding. Her pyjama top is wet with milk, the bottom with pee. There are even splashes of milk in her hair. Unable to scold her, I begin cleaning up, still in my pyjamas.

And yet I never learn: I go on sleeping in on Sundays. I go for every minute I can get. I continue to meld my body into the bedclothes, believing the tiredness will vanish if I give it just a little longer.

That morning, too, I'd got up cursing my daughter for not wanting to linger like me in the world of sleep. By the time I'd tidied up and finished preparing a breakfast that also served as lunch, it was after one o'clock. If I did the pile of laundry, the shopping, and the cleaning, it would be time for dinner. There was some ironing and mending too. The very thought made me so tired I sank down again onto the tatami. Would this Sunday go by, like all the others, without a single thing happening? I felt myself waiting for something, more wearily than eagerly by now. I knew my hopes would be disappointed again. Just because it was

Sunday, that didn't mean company around the table. The meal would be the usual tête-à-tête with my daughter.

As I watched a variety show on TV, unable to face the dishes, she was quick to take me to task: 'Why are you going back to sleep? It's Sunday today, it's not like other days.'

Soon, she hit on going out. 'It's boring at home, nobody's here. Let's go for a walk.'

After I'd taken no notice of this for a while, she began whimpering that she was lonely and bored.

We went downstairs and, once outside, she said gaily, 'Let's go to the wood. Let's go to Boolony Wood.'

'Boulogne!' I answered just as gaily. It was a waste: we'd moved in near a famous garden, which I jokingly called the 'Bois de Boulogne,' and we'd even been enjoying a glimpse of its greenery every day for months, yet we'd never gone there. Maybe a stroll in the park would have the makings of a real Sunday. The trees, the stretch of pond. The odours of earth and grass.

'Shall we go and have a look, then? I'll bet there are plenty of people out enjoying this great weather.' I took her hand in mine and set off. It was about ten minutes' walk to the garden's main gate.

I could see no sign of my daughter beside the pond, nor on its surface. On the lawn, several families were soaking up the warm sunshine with picnic lunches spread before them.

Three rather grubby ducks were being fed by a father with a toddler. People nearby were playing catch.

I hurried away into the woods. There, too, groups were seated in a circle on plastic groundsheets, tucking into packed lunches. Songs and laughter rang out. I found a bench that wasn't taken and sat down: it was too late to get into a panic now, I thought. I needed a cigarette, but I had only my wallet on me and I didn't dare ask a stranger for one of theirs. I stared at a smoker, gazed at the groves of trees, then at the ground by my feet. A speckle of shiny objects caught my eye. I leaned closer, wondering what they were: the pull-tabs of juice cans.

A boy of my daughter's age came running up to me. By the time I'd sat up straight, wondering what he wanted, he had run off again. He stopped by the reclining occupant of another bench and looked back at me. He seemed to be laughing. I stood up and went over. I'd seen the woman who was lying on the bench once before. I smiled at the boy, but then kept going: I didn't know his name, nor did I know his mother well enough to disturb her rest.

I had seen her at a daycare parents' meeting two or three weeks earlier. Having been late myself, I'd been relieved when someone else arrived after me. A face I hadn't seen before. I guessed her child must have started in April. Her clothes were rather mannish – a dark-brown T-shirt and jeans – but on her they just brought out her femininity. She had a fair complexion and symmetrical features. One of the staff asked her about her son's behaviour at home, and I could tell from her answer that she was on her own too. But while remaining very aware of these new arrivals, I hadn't run into the woman again, mornings or evenings, until that day.

As I moved away from the bench, I was oddly agitated about whether she'd have remembered me if I'd spoken to her. There was no reason she should. I hadn't said anything back then that suggested I lived apart from my child's father. I had yet to inform the daycare staff, in fact. But might my face have seemed vaguely familiar?

'Now where was it we met?' she might say. I would remind her, then ask, as an afterthought, 'Are you on your own too? Did your husband pass away? Or . . .'

I had a feeling she would give me a straight answer.

As I took a narrow uphill path out of the wooded area, I was still imagining the chat we would have. I was tremendously impressed by the calm of a woman who could fall asleep on a bench in a wood while her small child was with her. Lying there, she had seemed free of whatever it was that was still plaguing me.

'It hasn't been long,' I'd say, 'but somehow I'm worn out already, being on my own. I just don't know how you do it. Right now, I've let my child out of my sight and I don't know where to start, this place is so big . . .'

'That's easy,' she'd say breezily, then she'd climb onto the bench and give a dashing whistle. My daughter would come smartly, like a retriever.

'That's how you call a child back,' the woman would laugh, and she'd teach me the whistle.

'Well, now,' she'd say, 'why don't we all play together? The garden doesn't close for hours. What shall we play?'

The children would clamour:

'Tag!'

'Drop the handkerchief!'

'It's a pity to waste this bench,' I'd suggest. 'How about off-ground tag?'

'Good idea.'

We'd begin to play. My daughter and I would work up a sweat at the game, something we hadn't done in quite a while.

'This is fun, don't you think?' the woman would ask me, dropping her voice, and I'd nod vigorously . . .

My steps gradually quickened as I continued up the pathway. The 'hill' was just a knoll, a miniature mountain with a teahouse at the top from which to enjoy the view, but the route did remind me of a mountain path with its hairpin turns and tree branches closing in from both sides. I reached the teahouse in less than five minutes. There I found my daughter, huddled asleep in a corner. I guessed she had cried herself to sleep.

The sight of her curled up suddenly reminded me of a boy who'd hidden in a corner of the school hall when I was a child. He stayed missing half a day, and the rumpus that resulted involved the whole school as not only the teachers but the children were sent out to search for him. Rather than hang back in the classroom and be scolded, but not really meaning to look, I went to the hall, which I chose simply as a wide-open area that seemed to offer the fewest nooks to hide in. But once there I heard an eerie groaning in the wings of the stage, coming from behind the curtain. I panicked and ran off as fast as my legs could carry me. I told no one. I wanted nothing whatever to do with those eerie groans. I waited numbly in the classroom for the others to return.

Before long, they started to troop back and let me know he'd been found. He was crying behind the curtain in the hall, crying because he'd injured his leg and couldn't move, crying because he'd peed his pants. What a dummy, they said, all he had to do was call out.

I agreed. Why hadn't he called for help? I decided he was weird and didn't give him another thought. In fact, though, wouldn't the child have felt so intensely alone that he was afraid even to call for help? So alone that he'd had to hide behind the red curtain when there was nobody there?

The boy changed schools not long afterwards. His leaving may not have had anything to do with the hall incident, but at the time I couldn't help feeling vaguely that it had. It seemed even more likely now.

'Up you get. You'll catch cold.'

I patted my daughter's shoulder. She sniffed hopefully and, instead of getting up, sagged against my knees.

'Oh dear. Well, then, stand up and I'll give you a piggyback.'

'Mm.' Her eyes still closed, she stood unsteadily.

'Upsy-daisy.' It was a while since I'd taken her on my back. She'd grown too heavy for me, painfully so. Straightening up under her weight, I felt giddy and staggered for a moment. But, I thought, from now on I had to do what fathers did for their children as well. I should start practising to be a father to her too at times. I began to descend the hill slowly, watching my footing. Having perhaps dozed off again on my back, my daughter was a warm, heavy lump.

'Upsy, daisy,' I chanted quietly in time with my steps. The scent of azaleas well past their best was stifling.

When we reached the bottom, I tried joggling her. There was no response. I rubbed my forehead and eyes, then walked on.

The woman on the bench in the wood was no longer there. The child was gone too. And the last of the people around were packing up. I lowered myself onto the bench, half thinking it still held traces of her warmth. My daughter sleepily murmured something I didn't catch. I lifted my head and took in the treetops. Unlike the zelkovas, they covered the sky densely. It was a dark wood seldom penetrated by the sun. How much courage would it take to spend the night there? There'd be not a glimmer of moonlight, let alone starlight. I suddenly thought I'd like to give it a try. At the same moment, my fear became real. There were probably plenty of people still lounging around the sunlit pond. I hurriedly stood up, took my heavy daughter on my back again, and headed in that direction. Something shone in the shadows behind me and I felt an oppressive sensation, as if the thing were trailing insistently after me. The light was small but burning hotly.

'Can you look and see if there's something behind us?' I asked my daughter, who was still groggy. Yawning, she looked around.

'There's nothing there.'

'What about people?'

'Yes, there's a man with glasses and an old lady and . . .'

'That's OK,' I broke in, disappointed.

'Is something scary coming?'

'Forget it, it's OK.'

I strode towards the sunlit pond.

'A wolf? A fox? A bear?'

'Shh. That's enough about that.'

'But is it a wolf? A fox?'

'A wolf, yes, it's a wolf. Now shush.'

'There's no wolf. You're weird, Mommy.'

'What a chatterbox! Time to get down now and walk.' My impatience was beginning to get the better of me again.

But my daughter, not minding, scampered off towards the pond. I ran after her, out of breath. A weeping willow stood at the point where the side path joined the main one. As it caught the rays of the sinking sun full on, its brightness was dazzling to eyes grown accustomed to the shadows. My daughter was jumping up and down, trying to grab one of the willow's dangling branches. All right, I would wow her by grabbing a whole bunch. Shading my eyes with one hand, I approached my daughter in the light.

That autumn, I heard that a fire had broken out in the apartment of the woman and boy we'd seen at the garden. They were unharmed, as it happened, but the fire had spread to the house next door, and there two victims had been found. It was in the papers, people said, but I hadn't noticed it. The boy had been playing with a lighter belonging to his mother while she was out at a bar where she was a regular. I learned several things about her from another mother at daycare then: that she was raising on her own the child she'd had by accident, that they lived in a six-mat room, and that, perhaps being in need of their help financially, she had various men friends who visited late at night. 'I often saw her child wandering around at all hours,' the other mother said, 'and I thought this won't do. I believe she did have an office job during the day, so it looked as if she was going to muddle through, but now it's come to this. She can't have any money. I wonder what happens about compensation in these cases.'

I found out from her exactly where the fire had been and went with my daughter to see for myself. The apartment building and two adjacent houses had burned to the ground. The few charred timbers left standing traced bold lines like an abstract painting against the clear autumn sky. The rest of the debris and contents had been taken away in the two days since. Neither the woman nor her child was there, of course, at the roped-off site.

Where would her room have been? As my eyes followed the black lines of the timbers, I wondered to myself whether this could have been the origin of the hot light I'd felt behind my back that day.

Still, I regretted that we hadn't been able to enjoy the brilliance of that willow together. The tree blazed in my memory.

That autumn, I went to the local municipal office to pick up the form to file for divorce.

A DREAM OF BIRDS

There were many people seated in the room. I wasn't sure what had brought them there, but my guess was a calligraphy class. Sheets of white paper were pinned up on the walls, displaying what looked like the pupils' work.

I heard my name called. A man had turned towards me. I went over to him. He was red in the face and his breathing was laboured: he'd been drinking.

'That's your handiwork, isn't it?'

With a jerk of his chin, he indicated one of the sheets on the wall. Although I didn't recall doing any calligraphy, I nodded, thinking it must be mine if he said so.

'What a mess. Hopeless. I'd give up if I were you. It's getting even me down.'

He groaned in distress. So there's no way out, I thought, and was suddenly so afraid of my 'work' that I clung trembling to the man, who reeked of alcohol. His body was as hot as a sick child's.

He groaned again. 'Ah! Can't you do something? I'm just not a drinker.' He went on groaning without another word, shoulders slumped and head lolling. The nape of his neck had a reddened, puffy look that reminded me of fish roe, and his hair and clothes were sweat-soaked.

I realized I was carrying a towel, a white bath towel, and began using it to dab the back of his neck. I had to watch carefully how much pressure I applied to make sure it felt good: not too strong, not too light, and it had to be steady. By dabbing so precisely, I hoped I could make him aware of how I felt. My actions gave me a dizzying sense of plummeting deeper and deeper. The sensation was a fierce joy.

Pleasure like this had been invading my dreams on and off ever since my husband and I began having late-night talks about separating. The dreams didn't feature any particular man. On waking I'd have to acknowledge to myself that these were men I cared nothing for in real life. Their faces and bodies were a sort of interchangeable costume. All they had in common was being male. In my dreams I was freely choosing men I barely knew – a teacher at the place I used to go for after-school tutoring, an older cousin, my math teacher in junior high, a still-adolescent-looking member of a club I'd belonged to at school – and doing different things with each, but the pleasure, that radiance that seemed made of fear itself, was always the same.

I woke to find myself pinned down by my daughter on the futon we shared: she had one foot on my chest and her cheek against my arm. Dammit, why did I have dreams like that? Now that I was awake I missed that joy, and this only made me feel worse. Why didn't I ever dream of joyfully hugging my child? I felt thwarted, unable to dream as I wanted. If dreams could be exhibits in a court of law, the verdict would go against me in short order: I had no right to take my daughter from her father and raise her as mine alone. *The mother frequently has dreams of a libidinous nature*: there was no refuting that. The pleasure they brought was too intense for me to disown them. The men always resembled sick children and we never made love, yet it could only be sexual pleasure I was enjoying.

My daughter's third birthday was approaching. She was born in June, during a break in the rainy season, on a fine day that was as hot as midsummer. I had gazed at the brilliant blue sky through the hospital window as I waited for the contractions to increase. She has luck on her side: those were the first words my husband and I exchanged, laughing, after she was born. The weather had been nasty for days on end before clearing up overnight.

It occurred to me that this birthday would be a good excuse to invite some people round. When she was born, a stream of visitors had arrived to congratulate us, starting the day we brought her home. They were mostly friends of my husband's, but every face leaning over the cradle wore a smile, and it made my own heart glad to watch my baby daughter sleep with these adults beaming down on her, day after day. I also recalled one by one the surprisingly long list of presents we'd amassed: the outfits, bootees, photo albums, hanging mobiles, music boxes . . .

For her third birthday I certainly couldn't invite anyone from my husband's circle, however well I'd known them, to say nothing of his family. How many of those well-wishers who'd beamed over her as an infant could I invite now? I began sifting through the memories for forgotten faces, briefly getting up my hopes only to dash them again and again.

Things had been going badly. My daughter had come down with the chicken pox that was going around at her daycare, and for over a month I couldn't leave her in the centre's care. Unable to take time off, I'd left her with my mother, but then my mother had been unwell herself and I'd been forced to miss work for the past week. My boss, Kobayashi, had recently gone to the hospital with cirrhosis of the liver, and a man named Suzui, who was due to retire from another section of the radio station, had been assigned to the library in his place. Kobayashi would not be returning to the library even after he got out of the hospital. I was told that this was his own choice, but if that was true it was even more disheartening.

Suzui was a quiet, meticulous man. There was nothing especially wrong with him as a boss, but having grown comfortable with Kobayashi over the past four years I now felt disoriented, as if my workplace had changed beyond recognition. I was right in the middle of having to adjust to Suzui's pace when my daughter caught chicken pox. Asking for time off meant explaining why I couldn't turn to my husband for help. Unlike Kobayashi, Suzui knew nothing about me yet, and it was humiliating to have to touch on my private life for the first time in this way. 'You'll be finalizing the separation, then?' he asked, and to my dismay I could answer only that I didn't know, that I wasn't going to wait indefinitely for my husband's decision but I wasn't yet ready myself either. I was afraid Suzui might have me transferred to another department while I was away: he surely couldn't be too pleased that his sole assistant was likely to be asking repeatedly for time off.

My mother was another person I couldn't face without embarrassment. I didn't want to live with her, and I felt guilty about it. Having run off and left her on her own to be with the man I eventually married, now that he and I were no longer together I could hardly go home to her like a runaway child. Going it alone might lead to some sort of deliverance: that was the simple, urgent hope I was holding on to. And it made me feel guilty around my mother.

She didn't reproach me for falling back on her if and when it suited me. On the contrary, when I avoided her, holed up with my daughter in our fourth-floor apartment, she would bring us home-cooked meals. Murmuring apologetically that sometimes one didn't much feel like cooking with only one adult to feed, she would set out dish after dish on the table – homely things like stuffed cabbage rolls, deep-fried chicken, spinach *ohitashi* – and then hurry away.

However, I couldn't bear the thought of just the three of us celebrating my daughter's birthday. That would be too humble and cheerless. It was a frightening thing to contemplate, because I could see that it might well be very comforting to bring together our solitudes – my mother's, mine and my daughter's.

I chose to invite three guests; I couldn't have come up with more anyway. Two were old friends of mine and the third I knew through our children at daycare. Until just a year ago all three used to come around often, and we'd included my husband in these get-togethers and had no secrets from one another. In fact, he had let slip to one of them, accidentally on purpose, that we were going to separate, before I'd begun to take what he was saying seriously. The three of them had remained in touch with one another, so that even after their visits tailed off they had kept up more or less with our movements. Once we were living apart, my husband would call one of them from time to time, seeking news of our daughter; the friend would then phone me with advice, analyse the reasons for our rift from one angle or another, and end by laying out her theories about life. This meant I had at least stayed in contact with these three, if only by phone.

On the eve of my daughter's birthday, I finally made up my mind to call one of them. When I'd first thought of inviting a few people over, I'd been happy at the idea that I could make those carefree, lively times reappear by myself. I'd enjoyed thinking of this and that, planning the menu and so forth: we'd better have a birthday cake, even if it wasn't very fancy, and I'd buy flowers, and enough paper cups for everyone. I was in a particularly good mood for a while, but I grew discouraged as I weighed how many guests would actually come. Maybe I should give up and have my mother hold a quiet party. Yet I couldn't give in gracefully. I told myself to wing it and not worry so much: even if only one person came, mightn't that turn out to be a source of unexpected pleasure?

But the first friend I phoned said she couldn't make it, her baby had a cold. 'You're supposed to invite the child's friends to a birthday party, you know,' she added, laughing. 'Instead of me, why not invite Fujino? I'll bet he's upset right now because he can't join you tomorrow to celebrate.'

I tried the next person I had in mind, who was married but didn't yet have children.

She too answered with a laugh. 'You do get funny ideas! I can't make it, my sister-in-law is coming over tomorrow. But listen, how are things? My husband was saying just the other day that you two really should think it over carefully, seeing as how you have a child. Especially as she's a girl.'

I was growing obstinate. I phoned the third and last person I'd had in mind. Although we saw each other almost daily at the centre, lately we'd had no chance to stop and talk. She was a nurse working on night duty and she wasn't home that night. Her husband answered. Usually I was at ease with him – the four of us had spent evenings drinking together – but now I felt strangely hesitant to speak. When he offered to take a message, I answered hastily, 'No, never mind,' and hung up.

By now it was after ten. My daughter would be able to go back to daycare the following week as her spots had cleared up, apart from the last remaining scabs, and she had gone to bed at nine looking forward to that day even more than her birthday. After making sure she was asleep and tucking her in, I grabbed my handbag and went out. I couldn't bear to be in the apartment in the state I was in. I felt crushed, and it did no good to object that I'd brought this failure on myself – me and my silly ideas. I did my best to shrug it off: if only I'd invited people sooner, or told them I wanted to see them instead of seizing on a clumsy excuse, I wouldn't have had my hopes deflated. But my legs wouldn't stop shaking. It had been so little to ask. And to think that I'd reached out so cautiously, so tentatively, yet even that hand had been brushed off. I walked along the pavement clenching my fists and glowering resentfully at the moving headlights of passing cars.

Crossing the square in front of the station, I took a street beyond it that sloped gently downhill, and at the point where it divided I went into a little bar. The small space, on the ground floor of a residential building, held a man whom I took to be the proprietor, a woman in a black lamé blouse, and two customers: a middle-aged man seated at a table with work documents spread before him and, at the counter, a dark-complexioned woman a little older than me. Taking a counter seat myself, I ordered a whisky and water. It was a quiet spot. A big aquarium of tropical fish cast a faint light on the wall. Both staff were intently watching a small television behind the bar.

At first I was too tense to look around in case it was obvious I wasn't used to visiting bars on my own, but when I did take a look at the other customers, the face of the woman next to me struck me as vaguely familiar. Did she remind me of someone I knew? Or perhaps she lived nearby and I'd come across her before? Once I began wondering, my glance tended to drift back towards her, and at such close quarters she was bound to notice.

She turned to me and said with some asperity, 'Yes?'

Startled at being addressed, I stammered an apology, adding that I had a feeling we'd met somewhere. I no longer thought I knew her, however, as it was only in profile that her features had given me that impression. She was without makeup, except for heavy eyeliner that drew attention to her eyes. These were large, with thick eyebrows, in a round face. Perhaps because she wore no lipstick, her lips appeared sallow. Like me, she was in sandals.

'If you live around here,' I went on, 'we might have seen

each other once or twice, mightn't we? I live on the other side of the station . . .'

She smiled at last and gave a slight nod. 'I live just around the corner. I don't often go to the other side of the station, except to the drugstore. You know the one I mean? I save their coupons.'

'Oh, so do I!'

The coupons suddenly broke the ice. We agreed that they were slow to accumulate and that even then the free gifts were nothing special, and yet despite knowing this, once you'd received your first coupons you got hooked. We burst out laughing. I perked up even more on hearing that she too worked in an office and that she passed through the station at almost the same hour of the morning as I did. When I exclaimed that perhaps our paths had crossed there every day, she said, 'If we hadn't met here, we'd never have been any the wiser, would we? That calls for a toast. Have one on me.' As she spoke she rounded her large eyes, whose blood-shot tinge indicated she'd had a few already.

I had never been able to hold my drink, and it began to affect me as soon as I started to keep pace with her.

She told me in an undertone that she was learning Sanskrit. 'I'm leaving soon for India and I'm not coming back. What's there to come back for? You should go to India too.' Then she murmured some unintelligible words. 'See? That was Sanskrit for "Dark is the night, let morning come." Not bad, huh? Nobody at the office knows. The boys can't stand me. I'm careful with money, because I've got my plans, so they call me a frustrated old maid. But let them think what they like, right? What do I care?'

She muttered more unintelligible words and doubled up with laughter. I now realized that she was about ten years older than I'd originally thought.

We refilled each other's glasses repeatedly, with increasing merriment. The woman declaimed in Sanskrit, I burst into song with extravagant gestures, and the bar owner, who had joined us, took up a guitar and provided an accompaniment. When I overdid it and fell off the stool, the painful jolt reminded me of my daughter.

'What time is it?' I asked the owner.

It was after midnight. I leaned towards my neighbour, swaying drunkenly. 'Listen, why not come over to my place? I have to go home, but I'm enjoying this. Come on, don't worry, there's only my child.'

I tugged on her arm. Reluctantly, she got to her feet and left with me. We both walked unsteadily, each belting out a different song. Multicoloured lights swarmed brightly and beautifully all around the station, and the road leading to my building glowed faintly red as it meandered through them, pulsing like a blood vessel.

'Here we are, my place is on the fourth floor.'

'Uh-huh.' She let out a sigh, not even looking up.

'Watch your step, the stairs are really steep.'

Just as I was about to start up them, pushing her ahead of me, someone grabbed me by the shoulders from behind. I looked around to find Fujino filling the doorway. He was breathing hard, his chest swelling.

'What the hell are you doing?' His voice was close to tears.

Drunkenness made me demand, in return, 'What the hell are *you* doing *here*?'

'What the . . . ? What have you done with her?'

'She's tucked up in bed, sound asleep. *Ciao* . . .'

I turned away with a little wave. At the same moment, he hauled me off balance with both hands. For a second I didn't know what had happened. I hit my head hard on the ground. Then I picked myself up with a groan and hurled myself at my husband, knocking him into the street and falling on top of him. I scratched his face, pulled his hair, tried to throttle him. I was quickly flung off. Again I hurled myself on top of him and again I was sent flying.

'That's enough, you disgusting drunk . . . Get inside! Fast! What a sight.'

I was on all fours in the street, unable to move. My stomach heaved and its hot contents poured out when I opened my mouth. I was wondering blearily what I had done. All I understood was not wanting to let go of my husband, because his body brought back such memories.

As soon as I stopped being sick I scrambled to my feet; he was not the only one conscious of appearances. He was already gone. Catching sight of the woman looking down at me, I went to the bottom of the stairs and, beside myself with anger, told her, 'Time to go home! The show's over. So go on, what are you waiting for? There isn't going to be any more.'

She tottered off without answering.

When I finally reached my apartment after lowering the entrance shutter and climbing the stairs, I hunkered down, covered my face, and cried. Not a single clear emotion came with the tears.

The following week, my daughter returned to daycare and I to the library. Some days my mother collected her for me. I hadn't been transferred, but the backlog looked like it would take me six months to catch up, and I had to put in a certain amount of overtime. I was grateful to my mother for picking up my daughter. I would arrive at my mother's around eight, to a clamorous welcome: 'It's Mommy! Mommy's here!' Then my daughter would tell me where she'd come in the race to finish lunch, which bit of herself she had grazed this time, who had quarrelled over what.

'We saw that old lady,' she added one day.

My mother nodded approvingly. 'She always calls out "Hello, Granny" and the old lady looks really pleased. The poor thing must be completely on her own, wandering around in that outfit.'

'I suppose so,' I answered noncommittally.

The old woman they were talking about invariably put in

an appearance somewhere along our route, mornings and evenings. Her long hair was unkempt and she was dressed in a slightly grubby *yukata* in which she evidently also slept. Even in winter, she went barefoot in wooden *geta*. She probably was on her own, since she was always loitering in the same area, empty-handed and seemingly at a loose end. Whenever my daughter spotted her along our way she would call out a bright greeting, and after we'd passed by she'd keep calling 'Bye-bye, Granny' till we turned the corner. The first time we saw her after my daughter's long absence from daycare, the old woman rushed up to us herself and said, 'Where have you been? I thought you must have gone away.' Embarrassed by her concern, I explained about the chicken pox and thanked her for asking. She smiled broadly.

'Then we'll still see each other. I'm so glad. I should've known such a fine girl wouldn't let a little sickness stop her.'

'That's right, I'm tough,' said my daughter proudly.

I was curious as to how my mother felt about the old woman. Widowed herself at a young age and now living alone, could she see things in the woman that I couldn't? I hoped that she could. Surely she must be able to. They didn't need to talk or clasp hands. They could commune with a look, with eye contact. I wanted to believe that solitude at least equipped a person to do that.

I began chorusing hello along with my daughter when we met the old woman in the mornings. Occasionally, I even let myself imagine that we two could go and live with her, because it cheered me up to expand the bounds of what I could think of as not impossible. After a while, though, the old woman no longer appeared on our route; perhaps this time it was she who had fallen ill.

Not long after my daughter's birthday, I had a dream of birds. Since that night, my husband had been phoning me and waylaying me outside the library or the building where I lived, abusing me then dissolving into tears. What the hell was I thinking, he demanded to know, and how could I hate him so much? I looked on in silence, ruefully aware that I didn't hate him at all, I was just too scared of him in this state to say anything.

I had dozed off at my desk.

There was a leafless tree. A bird of a large tropical kind with a rosy face and green feathers flew down and perched on a branch.

A nearby voice murmured, 'Caged birds have been escaping. An increasing number of Nyasa lovebirds have gone wild.'

'Ah, Nyasa lovebirds . . .'

One more alighted on another branch even as I spoke. Yes, they were obviously on the increase, and in the time it took me to observe this they streamed down till the tree was covered in lovebirds. In the crush of gorgeous plumage, feathers plumped to the ground like overripe fruit.

Of all the birds it could have been, why had these particular creatures got out of hand? Were they so much fitter? In the dream, the question filled me with fear.

THE SOUND OF A VOICE

The hot days of summer were suddenly upon us.

The windows on every side of the apartment now stood open all day while I was at the library, and all night long as well. With nothing to act as a windbreak the rooms were almost too airy, and often at night the hem of the fluttering curtain would tickle my face. Once I came home in the evening to find the paper lampshade collapsed in a crumpled heap on the red kitchen floor after being batted down and tumbled about by the wind. The curtains I was sure I'd drawn in the six-mat room were half open, riding the wind, flapping and dancing. A flowerpot I used to keep on the sill was overturned as well. The unwatered soil, dry as sand, was scattered across the tatami, and the plant, which had died some weeks ago, lay on its side, its root fibrils stiffly extended.

It was a scene that, for a moment, inevitably suggested an intruder other than the wind. But after spending a winter and a spring in these rooms, though I'd felt far from secure when spring first arrived, by the summer I had started to have a sense that I needn't fear any break-ins by flesh-and-blood people. Whenever I looked down at the street four storeys below, I thought: who on earth would go to the trouble to scale those vertical walls, at the risk of their life? Surely no one so much as glanced up and noticed the windows.

Instead, living at that height meant it was a long way down.

One day, through an open window, I spotted a patch of bright colours like a burst of flowers on the tiled roof next door. The one-storey building housed a small, antiquated sweetshop, where a thin old man, who wore a black earflap hat even in summer, and his diminutive wife, who was both child-sized and bent, took turns sitting in the store by the light of one bare bulb. There was no sign of any other family member. I had bought candies there at my daughter's insistence several times, but they were always faintly dusty, and when they made a sale the old couple would give their wares a careful wipe with a cloth before handing them over.

Seeing the store's roof from the fourth floor after making these purchases, I would notice broken black tiles left unmended and weeds growing on the side that caught the sun. One couldn't help feeling that the old house was very near the end of its days.

The unexpected sight of bright colours on that weathered tiled roof set my heart racing with sudden foreboding. I leaned out of the window and took a closer look. They were coloured paper squares. Red ones. Blue ones. Green, yellow . . .

I could only conclude that every sheet in the pack of origami paper I had bought my daughter a few days earlier had floated down, one after the other, taking its time and enjoying the breeze, onto the tiled roof below. I pictured a small hand plucking one square at a time from the pack, reaching out the window, and releasing it in midair. My daughter, who had just turned three, would have been laughing out loud with pleasure as she watched the different colours wafting down.

When I was a child, a pupil had fallen from the rooftop terrace at my school into the yard. Not that I had witnessed this; it was a story that circulated among the children. He fell, but he supposedly, by a fluke, escaped without a scratch, landing neatly in a trough of water that was just big enough to take him. It was a cistern for firefighting, and even a child could see how small it was – it must have been about a foot across. For the longest time I had believed the story and marvelled at the boy's luck, but was such a thing really possible?

The children might well have made up that version of events. Maybe one of them saw the accident victim's body, noticed the nearby cistern, thought 'If only he'd landed in there,' and in a moment of anger at the child who hadn't fallen where he should, decided to forget he was dead. Reality couldn't be as brutal as that. Perhaps the child who saw returned to his playmates, not giving the body with its shattered skull a backward glance, and reported: 'They say someone fell off the roof, but he fell right into the water and he's fine,' adding, with a laugh, 'Some people do the weirdest things!' Yes, I remember the rumour as always being accompanied by laughter. The children had realized that it was possible to survive a fall from a roof, despite the grown-ups' best efforts to scare them, and the shared sense of superiority this gave them made them erupt in laughter.

All the same, around that time I began to dream of long falls. Often I was the one falling, my body being sucked into dark reaches like an absence of space, but I also dreamed repeatedly of other people – classmates, or family – plunging over some unknown height. It could have been a precipice; it could have been the school roof. The bottom was out of sight far below. They would take a jaunty step and then, all of a sudden, they'd be gone. Without nearing the edge I would listen hard. The length of the silence equalled the depth of the abyss. I counted: one second, two seconds, three seconds. Four . . . five . . . six . . . It was so deep I would be gripped by sadness. But eventually a sound would travel back from below. It was brittle, like breaking glass, but higher pitched, clearer, a beautiful sound. That, for me, was the sound of human bones shattering, and I couldn't relax till I'd heard it.

Those dreams of falling had stopped at some point, I wasn't sure when. Even now that I lived in a solitary tall building, I never dreamed of falling.

Several days after noticing the coloured papers, I looked

down at the neighbours' roof and saw another drift that had collected there, this time consisting of dollhouse furniture, little dress-up figures and toy blocks – flurries of my daughter's merry laughter, sparkling on the housetop.

I had a phone call one night. It was late and I was already in bed. The caller said she was a friend of my husband's; in fact, I remembered him mentioning her name shortly before we split up. He was talking about launching some sort of new project with this woman. She was a stripper in her forties. Apparently he had met her while working as a stagehand at one of the big cabarets.

It had been her own idea to call, she said politely, and would I please not say anything about it to Mr. Fujino?

My husband had abruptly broken off contact with me early in the summer. He had been phoning or showing up where and when I least expected him, accusing me of keeping our daughter from her father, of making no effort to give her a loving environment but going off to bars at night and drinking myself into a stupor, of always being on the lookout for some action. Just once, unable to bear it any longer, I had pleaded with him, between sobs, to leave me alone for a while. 'When you're like this I can't think, I'm too afraid of you, I can't take anything in. I'm worn out.'

At the time, he had told me I had only myself to blame and started with the insults again, but when I noticed the gap between his calls lengthening, I did wonder at first whether he could possibly have taken my appeal to heart at some later moment. That seemed unlikely, though. I was nothing to him now but an object of hatred. For his daughter's sake he was going to have to make me fall into line, to lock me into orbit.

After explaining that it was only with the greatest reluctance that she was becoming involved in other people's affairs, his friend began to speak her mind:

'Mr. Fujino and I have just spent a long time working together, so I couldn't help hearing about what's happening between you. I know all about it, I have to admit. Please don't be offended. I can see he's in real pain, and because I've been through a divorce myself it pains me to see him like that. So we've been talking things over, and maybe it's none of my business but I just had to tell you how I feel. The more I hear, the more it could be the old me he's talking about, and I've taken a real liking to you. You're very like me when I was young, you know. So I hope you'll accept a word of advice from someone who's been there. I got a divorce fifteen years ago. At the time, I didn't let it get me down, I told myself I was better off without the jerk, I could live the way I wanted, everything was turning out rosy. I wasn't a bit afraid. I was young, for one thing . . . And now, not a day goes by that I don't regret the divorce. It's been downhill ever since. I never did meet a man who'd make a better partner than my ex. But there's no going back. It still hurts, and that's why I just had to call you. You mustn't separate. You don't really hate him, do you? Any more than he hates you. It's obvious how deeply he loves you. Don't split up over some silly thing! You'll never find another man like Mr. Fujino. Nothing good will come of a divorce. Certainly nothing better than you have now, I can tell you.'

Before hanging up, the woman insisted I write down her number, promising me a sympathetic ear anytime.

About ten days later, I received a call from a professor who had mentored my husband as an undergraduate. He wanted to talk to me, in person, and hoped I could spare the time. I had met him on several occasions in my husband's company. He had a quiet manner that set me at ease.

We made an appointment at a restaurant during my lunch hour. The professor said: 'No doubt there are circumstances no one else is privy to, but perhaps you should calm down a little and listen to what young Fujino has to say. There are several divorcées among my own circle, and it's turned out to be a sad mistake in every case. Believe me, nothing goes right for a woman on her own. I'm only thinking of your happiness, and Fujino's. That's my only concern. And therefore I wouldn't rule out a divorce. But I think I know people pretty well, and I can assure you: you won't meet a better man than Fujino. The type of man you'll meet will go steadily downhill. That's a given. You have nothing to gain. Every woman thinks it's going to be different for her, but she ends up at the bottom of the heap all the same. There's no way around it. Take my advice and give up any thought of divorce.'

I met each of these remarks meekly with a nod.

As my boss Suzui had called in sick that day with a summer cold, I left to collect my daughter from daycare a little early. The place was usually deserted by the time I got there, but that day there were a good many children still waiting. At the entrance, a mentally handicapped boy was stroking the remaining outdoor shoes in their pigeonholes, one by one, with a long, slender leaf that he held in his hand. He was an appealing child, with a pale complexion and large eyes. But he almost never turned this sweet face to an adult, except for his mother, and the sound of his voice seldom passed those lips. His eyes, though, always held a mischievous sparkle. Instead of looking at people, he gazed with obvious pleasure at the light pouring over their bodies.

I had heard that it was at the centre, where he'd started as a baby, that they had noticed he wasn't developing normally, yet by that point they could hardly refuse him and they had kept him in their care, feeling they had no other choice. But the boy didn't like being cooped up and tended to putter around in the hallway or near the stairs just inside the entrance, where I often saw him. That day too I gave his familiar figure a passing glance, then promptly forgot him.

Later, however, as that encounter took on a special significance for me, I couldn't help feeling sorry that I'd missed my chance to look into those eyes of his and remember what I saw.

That night the boy would fall from the tenth floor of a housing complex to his death. No cistern was there to save him.

Three hours before this happened to the boy, I picked up my daughter and we stopped off at our fourth-floor apartment. Usually, I was in a rush to prepare dinner, but that day, perhaps discouraged by the professor's words over lunch, I didn't feel like setting to work. Pausing only to toss a bag of daycare things that needed laundering onto the kitchen floor, we went out to the Korean barbecue place on the other side of the street. We dined there once a week. Their big colour TV allowed me to eat at leisure and not worry about keeping my daughter entertained. I always ordered the set menu for me and a bowl of *gukbap* – rice and toppings in beef broth – for her.

As we were finishing our meal, a family came in wearing *yukata*. Both the parents and their daughters were dressed in the cotton summer kimonos, and the little girls each carried a water-filled balloon yo-yo and a funny mask. I remembered then that it was festival day at the neighbourhood shrine.

I hurried my daughter along and we headed over there. The nearer we got, the more people we saw in *yukata*, and both of us quickened our steps excitedly. The lights of the vendors' stalls came into view. So everyone was here, I thought. I was happy not to have been left out.

The grounds were as crowded as I expected, and the stalls were crammed in along the pathways, also just as I expected. There was a big tent with the usual sideshows as well. Balloons, pinwheels, yo-yos all glistened warmly in the light of the strings of naked bulbs.

My daughter and I scooped tiny goldfish into a plastic bag, we fished for water balloons, we had a try at the shooting gallery. We ate gaudy shaved ice and licked syrupy apricots on sticks. We bought a few dollhouse trinkets and some fireworks. Once we'd done a circuit, which was all too soon, it was a matter of repeating ourselves; there were no more surprises to be had. Nothing remained to be seen, however hard we looked.

I went into a dark corner of the grounds to have a cigarette. At the sight of its glow, my daughter wanted to set off the fireworks we'd just bought, there and then.

'OK, but only the little ones,' I said and, taking the bundle of sparklers from the plastic bag for a start, I gave her one to hold and lit it for her with my lighter.

'Now don't move your hand, you have to keep very still,' I instructed, showing her how to tilt the delicate twisted-paper stick downwards.

She stood with her arm held out stiffly, intent on the fire with which she'd been entrusted. A ball of it gradually began to swell at the sparkler's tip. The bigger the tip grows, the more splendid the display it produces once it starts to sparkle, but the more likely it is simply to drop off under its own weight before giving out any sparks at all. The tip of my daughter's swelled steadily, then began to spark vigorously. But as it did, her hand wavered and the fireball fell to the ground.

'Oh, that's a shame! All right, have another try. And I'll do one too this time.'

I gave her another stick to hold and took one in my own left hand, then lit them both at once. Mine initially let out some showy sparks and formed a large globule, but then flopped. My daughter's, though smaller, kept going. She was holding her breath; I did the same, and we watched as the sparks dwindled. When the small ball dropped off at the finish, she gave a disappointed sigh.

'That one did well, didn't it?'

'It fell off.'

'They're supposed to, sweetie.'

'I want another one.'

'Then see if you can beat me again. This time I'll really try,' I said, handing her a new stick.

'Oh, how nice, can we join you?'

A voice spoke suddenly above my head. I looked up in surprise: it was the mother of a daycare classmate of my daughter's. Her little girl had already crouched beside mine.

I'd barely spoken with the mother till now, but my daughter mentioned the child's name practically every day. Both the mother and her daughter were dressed in *yukata*.

'Why don't we all have a sparkler competition?' she went on.

'Sure, help yourself.' I held out the bundle in my lap, but she shook her head with a smile and pointed to the plastic bag her child was carrying, which was quite full of fireworks. She took out their sparklers, gave one to her child, and took one herself. I lit the four sticks at once with my lighter. As we crouched in a circle, our four faces were bathed in a faint red glow. My stick again developed a good-sized fireball. The little girl's dropped off first, then her mother's. I began to hope that mine might keep sparkling to the last this time, and my heart pattered. But no, mine fizzled out too. Once more, my daughter's outlasted us all.

'Again!' she cried, throwing the spent stick away. She was breathing hard. 'Quick!'

'Hang on, let's try a different kind. Look, how about this? It says it's a "Spark Shooter."' There was no guarantee her sparkler would last the longest three times in a row, and I was worried about her disappointment when she lost.

'No! I want to do these!' she answered loudly, reaching and grabbing the remaining sparklers from my knee. The other mother laughed.

'My, what a fierce look! Is it getting time for beddy-byes?'

'I'm not sleepy! Here, everybody have one.' She pressed a

sparkler against the chest of her friend, who took it without protest.

'Here, this is for you!' The child's mother accepted, chuckling.

'Mommy too!'

'There's no budging you, huh? The other fireworks are calling, "Hey, what about us?"'

'I don't care.'

I flicked my lighter and four more sparklers caught alight.

'You know, festivals really were more fun in the old days,' the child's mother murmured, for no particular reason.

'That's because we were children,' I answered, watching my fireball begin to grow.

'I wonder. Were you born in Tokyo too?'

'Yes.'

'I've been coming to this festival since I was a child . . . You could be right, I suppose. Somehow, though, I think it's more than that . . . When I come here now, I feel kind of cheated. Growing up is overrated, if you ask me. If I'd known adult life would be this boring, I'd have had more fun while I could. Lately I wake up in the morning and I just feel so blah . . . But I still have to go to work at the store . . .'

'It's all downhill, you mean.' Recalling the professor's words earlier in the day, I started to laugh.

'I do love fireworks, though. Just give me some fireworks to watch and I'm happy.'

The ball fell off my sparkler. My daughter's dropped next

and the other mother's dropped almost simultaneously, leaving the little girl's, though it didn't last much longer either. My daughter started to cry.

'It's because you mommies are making too much noise. You have to be quiet.'

At that instant, through her crying, I thought I heard a distant scream. A voice that seemed to plummet. A voice whose sound obliterated the ground beneath my feet, turning it to murky darkness. Instead of attending to my daughter, I stood up and listened.

'Mommy! Mommy!'

'What is it?' asked the other mother. 'Has something happened?'

I nodded. I didn't know what, at that moment, but I nodded as if I were certain.

At daycare the next morning, I learned of the boy's accidental death. My throat tightened at the thought of the scream I'd heard: so it was him. It seemed he had been playing alone on an outside walkway, and he had gone over the railing.

What was he seeing as he fell with that cry? It was nighttime; the glow of streetlamps, lighted windows, and neon signs must have streamed like water around his falling body. Perhaps he gazed in amazement at the unfamiliar torrent of lights, wondering where he was going. That yell did seem more like a whoop than a scream, now that I thought about it.

I didn't let anyone know that I had heard the boy's last cry.

———————

The windows of my apartment stayed wide open all summer.

My daughter continued to drop her possessions out of the window onto the neighbours' roof when my back was turned. Praying she wouldn't take it into her head sooner or later to try dropping herself, I still couldn't bring myself to have a showdown.

THE MAGIC WORDS

My daughter cries and cries. In my sleep I curl up, my back to the sound. Muffled by her crying, brief dreams succeed one another, dim as magic lantern slides.

Fluorescent-red rambling roses are flowering away along a hedge. Feeling quite blissful, I am about to pick a rose . . .

It starts to rain and I can't leave the station . . .

My daughter lies on a green table. I am in tears. 'You're her mother, why were you late to pick her up? This would never have happened if you'd been on time, I knew I should have kept her,' her father sobs, shaking her body . . .

The crying fell into place. Conscious of my daughter's cries at last, I opened my eyes. They were wet. I checked the clock: it was 2:30. These nightly crying spells of hers tended to start at the same times, around two and again at dawn. They had been going on for nearly a month now. I couldn't have said exactly when they began; by the time I realized it, she was having them regularly, and wetting the bed as well. As my sleep was interrupted night after night, the sight of her crying would rile me till I felt more like slapping her cheek than taking her in my arms, and although I managed to control my hand, I would snap at her unthinkingly.

'How can I sleep with that noise? Do you have any idea what time it is? That's enough! Come on, can't you tell me what's wrong? How am I supposed to know if all you do is cry? Well, tough, then.'

She cries harder at this. Even more riled, I shove her aside.

'OK, so you've wet the bed again. What's up? You never used to. Come on, stop that now, it doesn't do any good. Will you be quiet!'

She sobs miserably, 'My pyjamas are icky! The futon's all wet!'

I pile on the blame. 'Don't be silly, you're the one who wet them. We're all out of pyjamas. And this is the only futon. Stay like that. And go to sleep now. Crying won't help. Did you hear what I said? Quiet down! What does it take for you to understand – a slap?'

She won't stop. Giving in, I stand her up, take off her pyjamas, cover the wet patch on the futon with a towel, then moisten a washcloth in the kitchen and apply it to cool her chest. Little by little, her rapid heartbeat calms. She clings to me, sniffling, and eventually falls asleep with her mouth open. As if finally coming to my senses at the sight of her sleeping face, I hurriedly begin to caress her head and her cheeks. I drop off too before I know it, but when her crying wakes me again at daybreak, I'll only do it all over again.

As the sleep-deprived days wore on, I would catch myself

nodding off at the library where I worked. By the time I rushed to collect my daughter from daycare in the evenings, I would be so drained of strength I could barely hold my head up. Yet once we set off for home, she would whine for an ice cream as we passed a candy store, dash out into traffic when she spotted a cat, and demand a piggyback before we'd gone far. I would gradually turn pale with vexed indignation: Was the child testing my endurance? Was she playing me for a fool, dragging me around like this? Her face resembled her father's. I would avoid looking at it, but grip her hand tighter. Once we got home, I would sprawl drowsily on the futon by myself, leaving her as much as possible to her own devices until bedtime. And in the middle of the night she would start to cry.

How to get her to sleep peacefully through the night was not my first thought. It was my own lack of sleep that worried me. I took to downing whisky before bed – more than my limit, in an attempt to stop myself being woken. But no matter how deeply under I might be, I would always hear my daughter's wails. My head thick with alcohol, her incessant crying was more exasperating than ever, so that rather than go on like this, I'd almost want to put the wet towel over her mouth and nose. Giving her a halfhearted cuff on the head instead, I would go and throw up in the sink and mutter, 'Help me, help me,' as I washed my face under the tap.

That night, too, I had drunk myself under. My daughter's wails resembled the sound of waves. Once I sat up, I realized she was still alive. I rubbed my bleary eyes and looked at her. My hands and legs were trembling, and inside me her father's grief had outlasted the dream. Reaching out, I touched her on the arm, on the back: they were hot and soft to the touch. She was alive. I wasn't sure which was real, which a dream. My wild-eyed hope for the daughter I'd seen dead seemed to have come true with startling ease, but even if I'd dreamed it, I was so grateful for her return that I had to embrace her living body, amazed that the blessing of my daughter being alive had been granted to the likes of me.

I don't know how long I held her – long enough to find she'd fallen asleep sucking on my pyjama sleeve. I laid her down, slipped off her pyjama pants and underwear and took them into the kitchen. The uncurtained kitchen window let in enough light from the neon signs and streetlamps outside to make the colours in the room distinguishable. After tossing the dirty laundry into the washing machine, I went up the stairs to the rooftop terrace. There were a number of lit windows visible even at that hour. I set about counting them.

For once, she slept soundly the rest of that night, without crying.

In the morning, she woke me by pulling my hair. A glance at the clock showed it was already past 8:30. I scrambled to get us both dressed, and after she'd had a glass of milk we were on our way. Impatient at her slow pace as we headed for daycare, I picked her up and ran. As I did so, the thought that, in spite of everything, maybe some part of me wished my daughter dead crossed my mind. Why would I have dreamed of her dead body otherwise? She was heavy. My arms grew numb and I could barely see ahead. I ran on as if clinging to her weight.

When we reached the centre, she tripped away to join the other children without a backward glance. The moment when she separated herself from me was a palpable relief.

We were entering our eighth month of life on our own together. The days were still hot, but the nights were growing chilly, and we had caught slight colds in turn.

All this while, I had kept hoping that once I settled into the new apartment – about the time I became able to find my way around it with my eyes closed and not bump into things – the normality of a relaxed and reasonably sociable existence like the one I used to have, back when I'd started living with my husband, would be conferred on me. That seems to have been my state of mind in those months. For all the world as though I were studying for an entrance exam, I guess I must have believed that if I did my best I would pass, after which I could coast, feeling proud of myself. I did start out with every intention of jettisoning my starry-eyed expectations and recognizing what I'd failed to see so far, but I didn't yet know what it meant in practice to trim my expectations.

There was no question that I now knew my way around

the apartment we'd moved into that winter, on the fourth floor of an office building. The kitchen's red floor, new when we moved in, was already looking dingy with the stains of the milk and the food my daughter spilled almost daily, the crayon scribbles, the traces of potty accidents. And the tatami mats had changed colour with time. Even the lint in the closet was a familiar sight.

And then she had started crying at night. It was not so much hearing her crying as finding myself shouting vile abuse and feeling like smothering her that made me realize for the first time just what the long days ahead would be like. I longed to have my old life back. But there was no going back now, nor any way out. I couldn't decide whether I'd done this to myself or fallen for a ruse of unknown origin. What I'd failed to see so far, it turned out, was my own cruelty.

'The goldfish died! The goldfish died!' The cry from my daughter had woken me one morning. The clock showed it was very nearly time to get up. I hauled myself out of bed and into the kitchen with her tugging me by the hand.

'Mommy, there, look. Over there.'

Her cheeks were flushed with excitement. She followed timidly behind me as I approached the spot she'd pointed out. The goldfish wasn't easy to see against the red floor. In the morning light, the little fish lay beside the plastic wash-basin we'd used as its bowl. Without its sole inhabitant, the water in the basin was perfectly still.

We'd brought the goldfish back from the local shrine's fair in the summer. It had been remarkably lively when we released it into the basin and, thinking it might live a month or so, I'd bought some fish food granules and together we'd fed it now and then. It was the first creature we'd kept in the apartment. And it had indeed survived a month, although I hadn't foreseen that its end would come with a leap out of the basin.

I placed the fish on my palm and held it up to my daughter's face. Its body was still soft.

'It really is dead. Here, touch it and see.'

Her eyes wide and mouth open, she brushed it with her right index finger. 'It's not moving . . . It's cold . . .'

She gradually grew bolder and, laughing as if being tickled, she tried pinching its dorsal fin and tapping its head with her nail.

'This is what happens when things die, you know. It's the same with people. The goldfish didn't know that, and it went and jumped out, kersplosh.'

'Silly goldfish,' laughed my daughter, seemingly delighted.

'Don't you feel sorry for it?'

'Uh-uh.'

'What shall we do with it? Pity to let it go to waste – shall we eat it?'

'Ugh!' she exclaimed, startled.

Keeping a straight face with some difficulty, I continued,

'Not like this, of course. We'd cook it in soy sauce. You never know, it might taste very nice.'

'Ugh. No! I'm not eating a goldfish. Quick, throw it away.'

'You're sure? OK, out it goes. Pity, it looks so tasty.'

'Do it quick!'

I discarded the goldfish in the vegetable-peeling container in the corner of the sink. Then I lifted my daughter up to let her see it lying among the scraps.

'It's not moving at all.'

'You got it. That's why dead things go in the garbage. You'd be like that too if you died, so don't you die, you hear me?'

She nodded, laughing.

Mine was the gaze that lingered on the goldfish's corpse, moving on only with regret. Had this been enough to distance my daughter a little from death?

Around that same time, I had received a phone call from the daycare centre just as my workday was coming to its close. In some agitation, the young teacher in charge of my daughter informed me that Fujino, her father, had taken her away.

'I'm afraid I may not have quite understood, but he simply dropped by to collect her, you see, and because I know him well by sight I thought that must be what you'd arranged for today, and I handed her over. I hope I did the right thing? In any case, I thought I'd better check . . .'

I practically jumped down her throat: 'Did he say where

they were going?' I half rose from my chair. Something told me this had been bound to happen sooner or later.

'No, he didn't say. Then it's what I thought . . .'

'What time was this?'

'No more than ten minutes ago. Oh, how awkward. But, I must say, this wouldn't have happened if you'd made the situation clear.'

'You could have asked. Why didn't you phone me *before* you handed her over?'

'How were we to know? It's not as if yours is the only child we have to look after.'

'I'm well aware of that. But . . . well, in any case, I'll go home immediately. If you hear anything, please contact me there.'

I put down the receiver and, with an apologetic bow to Suzui, my supervisor, who was staring at me, I ran out of the library, leaving catalogue cards scattered on my desk. I thought of a taxi, but at that hour the train would probably be quicker. I descended the station stairs at a run and sat shaking on the train.

I made it home in half an hour. Only when I opened the door and saw the place empty did I realize that rushing home hadn't brought me any closer to my daughter. My apartment would give me no clue as to where Fujino was taking her. But it made no sense to race over to the centre now either. I hadn't a hope of picking up their trail in the streets; I could only wait where I was, after all. I didn't even know where

Fujino was living. I'd gathered that he had moved in with a certain woman, but I wasn't sure of this. He had changed his address twice since we separated. That much I had heard directly from him.

In a daze, I sat down at the table and waited. I was unable to act or to think. I couldn't bring myself to curse Fujino or to assume the worst – that he'd snatched my daughter. Time had stopped. I had lost consciousness with my eyes open. I could have gone on waiting like that for days, or indeed for years.

Time restarted when a knock at the door made itself felt. Lunging like an avalanche from a great height, I flung the door open.

'Mommy! Here I am. It's Daddy. We went for a walk, Daddy and me.' Her voice ringing with excitement, my daughter came bouncing towards me. Thrown off balance as I caught her, I leaned against the wall and gave her a hug. Her body was radiant. The dazzling light obscured everything around her. Placing her behind me, I looked out the door, where there was a dark shadow.

'Hi. Just the thing for a beautiful day like today. Hey, no need to look so grim, I brought her right back, didn't I?'

I went up to the shadow and slapped it with all my might. I felt its body warmth through my palm. His cheek was warm. Keeping my eyes on Fujino, who stood there dumbstruck, I felt my tears well over like the juice of squeezed fruit.

Before he could open his mouth, I slammed the door and

locked it. I couldn't turn around. Behind me, my daughter stood motionless, not making a sound. With my face to the door, I took care not to let sobs escape my throat. Fujino knocked for a while, but after one final loud thud – a kick, perhaps – he stormed down the stairs. All was quiet behind my back. Though I longed to hold my daughter, I couldn't stem the flow of tears.

How long did I stay there at the door? It was she who made the first move, wrapping her arms around me from behind and asking in a whisper, 'Mommy . . . What are you looking at? Daddy isn't there anymore.'

I nodded, then turned around, and we went back inside. Stopping by the sink, I unlaced her hands from around my hips and stood her in front of me. Once I'd wiped my face and blown my nose on a towel, I hugged her close.

'My head hurts. I banged it,' she mumbled as if to herself, turning her face away.

'Does it? Then let's say the magic words: "Ouchie, ouchie, fly away."' My voice shook as I spoke the playful children's incantation, while she watched my lips out of the corner of her eye.

The head of the daycare centre asked if she could have a few words as I was about to pick my daughter up the next evening. 'There's nothing harder on the child than leaving things dangling. For your little girl's sake, as well as your own, the sooner you reach a decision the better, whatever it may be. Until things are settled, we'll make it a rule not to hand your daughter over to her father, but if he were to force his way in here and refuse to take no for an answer, there's nothing we could do. Our staff are all women, for one thing, and we have no legal basis to turn him away. May I ask what your own plans are? I'm sure it's not easy to discuss this, but we do need to know a little more if we're to be confident about having her here. Up to now, we haven't seen any obvious changes in her behaviour, but . . .'

I replied that I wanted to get a divorce and bring up my daughter myself, and that I thought her father would probably agree to that, but I didn't yet know what to do about their seeing each other. He evidently wanted to be able to see her whenever he liked, but I couldn't accept that arrangement, because why had he left us, in that case?

'Then, for now, you don't want her to see him?' the director asked.

'Whatever we may decide in the future, for now I'd rather she was left in peace . . . I don't want him unsettling her. Or does a child really need to continue seeing her father?'

'It depends,' she replied, 'but, on the whole, it does seem to be better, for the child's sake, not to arrange meetings with the parent who leaves. That doesn't mean avoiding all contact, but it does seem to be the safer course.'

'I see.' I hung my head: this was not the complete reassurance I had hoped for.

As she rose to her feet, the director tried one last time to ascertain how I felt. 'You have no wish to live together again, then?'

When I shook my head, she said, 'Very well. We'll do what we can to assist, as you are her guardian at present. So take heart, and do take good care of her. For her sake.'

The onset of my daughter's nightly crying spells was surely related in some way to the day I slapped Fujino's cheek, though I couldn't for the life of me remember the exact timing.

A couple of nights after I'd dreamed of her death, as she cried and cried, the same as ever, I laid her on my lap like a baby and began to recite 'magic words' while rubbing her chest and stomach, tracing circles.

'Bad dreams, go away. Nightmares, leave this child alone. She's a good girl, let her have only good dreams. Hear my plea . . . May the bad dreams go away. May nightmares leave this child alone. She's a good girl, let her have only good dreams. Let her have happy dreams, full of pretty flowers. Let her dream she's dancing, wearing lovely clothes . . .'

My daughter had stopped crying and was listening to my voice, a smile on her lips. Encouraged by that smile, I continued, still more fervently, to recite the magic words.

THE DUNES

The installation was over in a couple of hours – so quickly I was taken aback. I saw the two young workmen out, bowing agreeably even as I wondered why I should be the one to feel apologetic. Then I turned: every window was covered, stiflingly, in brand-new blue mesh.

'Our house has gone blue. I can't see outside.' My daughter ran around the dining-kitchen as she'd done the first time we came to the apartment.

'It can't be helped. It could have been worse – at least they haven't blocked the view completely,' I answered as I gazed out of a window through whose blue mesh everything appeared in a thick fog.

About ten days ago, the old man from the neighbouring sweetshop had appeared at my door in a rage. I was just giving my daughter her dinner of spaghetti with meat sauce out of a can. Since she was still not great at feeding herself, if we ate together her meal would take up all my attention and

I'd get nowhere with my own, so I usually fed her, then sat down to my dinner. That was the moment of my day I looked forward to the most. I took a simple delight in satisfying my hunger, which since around five o'clock had gradually been turning into an ache. But the meal was always over in no time, and the delight with it.

I had answered the door with some irritation, wondering who it could be at that hour, and then smiled, reassured, on finding our elderly neighbour standing there. I had a feeling he would be bringing good news. He was a gruff and rather grumpy old man, but he didn't strike me as narrow-minded, and I made a point of greeting him politely whenever I saw him. The day I moved in, he had explained about the garbage pickup, and when he once asked about our household and learned I was on my own with my daughter, he'd said, 'That must be hard. Anything you need to know, don't hesitate to ask.' I had greeted him all the more politely from then on, and I felt he was one person I could count on to have a passably good impression of me.

But the moment he saw me that night he launched into a tirade, his cheeks quivering and voice shrill. Not following at first, I regarded his pale face, nonplussed. Still more incensed, he waved his fist and yelled, 'Don't play dumb with me! You take me for an old dodderer, don't you? Well, you're not fooling me with that innocent look. Wrecking people's houses – you know exactly what I'm talking about!'

At last I remembered that since the summer my daughter had been amusing herself by dropping things onto the old man's roof. I had scolded her whenever I caught her at it and had done my best not to let her near the windows by herself, but with no one else to keep an eye on her she'd had plenty of chances. I'd been inclined to overlook a few such mishaps as unavoidable, feeling sure that before long her interest would shift elsewhere. And, in fact, with the arrival of autumn I'd been leaving the windows open less often, and she did seem to have forgotten about dropping objects out.

'She's dropped something again, hasn't she?'

'Hah! You're willing to admit it, now, are you?'

Still not quite understanding why he was in such a rage, I went inside in some alarm, opened the kitchen window, and looked down. It was difficult to tell in the dark, but it was true that more things had collected in a drift on the roof below. As I tried to see if she'd done some damage, perhaps made a hole, the old man joined me and surveyed his roof.

'Ah, what a mess . . .'

'I'm sorry. I did try to watch out.'

'What, with all that down there?'

'I'm really very sorry.'

'Oh no, you're not getting off with just an apology.'

'. . . I'm sorry.'

'I know you couldn't care less about a dump like that, but you listen to me. Us two old dodderers live in that house and we're just minding our own business, my wife is laid up, and there's all this thundering that comes out of nowhere above her bed. She can't sleep a wink. To say nothing of the leaks . . . Have you any idea how much roof repairs cost? Well, anyhow, come on down. The missus is waiting.'

As the old man watched, I lifted my daughter from her chair, whispered, 'You can eat later, this is important, so be good now,' and slipped on my sandals.

His little wife was standing in their dark store, wearing a quilted jacket. I bowed as deeply as I could and apologized. It was useless to offer excuses, I was clearly in the wrong. I had focused solely on my daughter dropping things and never given a thought to the people underneath startled and frightened by the thuds above their heads. I'd actually derived some comfort from the fact that the black tiled roof, rather than the street and its pedestrians, was directly below.

Taking turns, the old couple told me with rising vehemence how they'd had to move their futons because of the leaks, how at first they'd feared it was some kind of disaster and even thought of evacuating the building, but being old and helpless they'd stood it as long as they could, and how they'd like to give me a taste of that terrible din. I bowed my head meekly at each accusation, making my daughter bow hers too. I promised to take care of the repairs, adding that they had only to let me know if there was anything else I could do.

They paid no attention, however, continuing to outshout each other in their excitement. I listened in silence, intending to accept whatever they said. It would take more to soothe them than settling the repair bill and uttering polite apologies. I hoped that my standing there letting their voices pour over me might help make amends. I stared at my feet, wondering forlornly when I'd get to go upstairs and sit down to my dinner.

'. . . I don't know what you've been dropping, but this little child could never have done all that by herself,' said the old man.

'She pretends it's the child when all this time she was behind it herself.'

'I wouldn't put it past her, the minx.'

'We've caught on to you and your ways, you see. We said to each other, something's bound to happen any day now! We're just lucky you didn't start a fire.'

'No decent woman could afford a place like that on her own . . .'

Let it go, let it go, I heard my voice tell myself, but before I could stop I spoke up: 'What do you mean, I pretend it's the child?'

The old man answered, 'Weren't you in on it too? Dropping stuff.'

I knew I should keep quiet, but I had to say one more thing: 'Do you really think any parent would do that?'

'Oh, there are all sorts of parents,' said the wife.

'What's that supposed to mean?' At that moment I lost my self-control. Though I was breathing with difficulty and my eyes were misting, there were certain things I owed it to myself to say. Plunging on, hardly aware what words were coming out of my mouth, I protested hoarsely that I realized a parent was responsible for her child's actions and I was truly sorry for what had happened, but I had never, ever thrown anything out the window myself, I was a parent, I wouldn't do a thing like that. How, I appealed, could I get them to believe me?

'Calm down, will you?' The old man's dismayed voice suddenly reached me, and I lowered my head and exhaled deeply. 'There's just no talking to you, is there? In any case, we won't stand for any more damage to our roof, so we're having wire mesh fitted over your windows. I went to discuss it today with your landlady, Mrs. Fujino, and I'm seeing her again tomorrow. My mind's made up. The decision doesn't involve you. All you have to do is get used to it.'

'Suit yourselves, I'm only a tenant . . . ,' I said in a small voice, then turned my back on the old couple and went home. They stood dully watching us go as if the confrontation had taken a lot out of them. As I climbed the three flights of stairs, I pictured my apartment with dark cages of wire mesh over the windows. It didn't seem possible.

My daughter, still in my arms, murmured with a sigh, 'That was scary.' I nodded, then the next moment, overcome with vexation, I burst out crying.

'Mommy . . . are you all right? Don't cry, there's a good girl.'

They were the words I so often said to her. I nodded over and over. 'You're right, I shouldn't cry over a thing like that . . . But, please, don't throw anything else out the window, OK?'

She nodded in turn. I looked up to see my apartment door standing open, as I'd left it, and a triangle of lamplight from inside illuminating the dark landing. I'm her mother, all the same, I thought. Even if I was an incorrigible fool, I wanted to believe that there was still something fundamental in me worthy of my own respect. I would have liked the old couple to believe in it too, but all I'd managed to do was screech and carry on. Although I'd brought it on myself, I felt dizzy with disappointment that they'd turned out to be no different from all the others.

About a week later, I received a call from the realtor who managed the building. After considering the alternatives, they had decided to cover the windows with netting to prevent accidents, and could I please be home on the day of the work? He added considerately, 'It's nylon mesh, so there should be hardly any effect on the view.'

'Which windows will be covered?'

'All the large ones,' replied the realtor. 'All except the kitchen and toilet.'

The workers came that Saturday afternoon.

Then, late the next night, a man by the name of Kawachi

phoned unexpectedly. He was at the station: would I mind if he came round, as he wanted to talk to me? Sure, I answered at once. It seemed only natural that Kawachi would come and see me. In fact, I'd almost got tired of waiting for him.

A while back, a young secretary at the radio station whose duties often brought her to the library had invited me over, with my daughter, and we'd ordered in sushi. Her place consisted of a six-mat room and a dining-kitchen half that size. She kept it much tidier than my messy apartment, so tidy it felt cold to me. Over several beers, I listened to the office politics she'd got involved in through the union. When my daughter began grumbling sleepily, we were invited to stay the night since it would be a pity to leave just when I'd got comfortable and a little mellow. Very relieved not to have to set off home with my daughter on my back, I started on the bottle of whisky I'd brought that evening.

I'd begun to get to know this colleague, who was two or three years younger than me, only after my separation from Fujino. As we gradually confided in each other, I learned she'd been seeing a married man for several years. When I told her about my situation, she sounded somehow disappointed. 'I guess that's why I started noticing you a while ago, then. That's too bad: I thought you were just an ordinary person.'

Laughing, I insisted I was very ordinary, as she could see.

'No, we're neither of us ordinary. Not now, anyway. That's probably why we get along so well, don't you think?'

Excited by my first night out in a long time, I downed a good deal of whisky as we chatted about this and that.

Stretched out on the tatami, I was just dozing off when her lover put in an appearance, completely out of the blue as far as I was concerned. I sat up, startled. My friend was objecting that he couldn't just show up, she had plans too, but it was more than I could have expected that she would actually turn him away for my sake.

'We've got quite a head start. Here, have a drink – make it a double or you'll never catch up. Have you called home? Use the phone if you want.'

Smiling, the man started dispatching a whisky without replying.

I ought to take my daughter and go, I told myself. Now that he'd joined us, I was a third wheel. But I couldn't get going. By now it was a huge effort to move, and furthermore I really couldn't see why I should be the one to leave when I was there first. But nor could I ignore the hints my friend was giving, as she nervously took care of both of us, that she'd rather I made myself scarce.

She refilled his glass repeatedly, and as the whisky rapidly took effect he began to dabble with her fingers while maintaining an amiable smile in my direction. He touched her breast, stroked her thigh. All of this seemed distinctly aimed at me. Did he suppose I envied her? I was starting to feel sick, and developing a headache.

'I just need to make a quick phone call,' I said, getting up.

'Go ahead. But who are you calling at this hour?'

I answered as offhandedly as I could, 'My lover, of course, who else?'

'Oh . . . Seriously?' She stared at me, puzzled. The man laughed, put his arm around her shoulders, and pulled her close.

Grabbing my diary from my handbag, I riffled through the addresses at the back. Any number would do: just dial. My fingertips shook. I came across Kawachi's name. He was the head of the parents' association at my daughter's day-care. He had spoken to me not long ago to ask why I didn't attend the meetings, and he'd written his home number in my book. 'Why don't you come round to our place some-time?' he'd said. 'Let's discuss it where we can say whatever's on our minds.'

Deciding I could probably get away with calling if I used this number, I dialled the barely legible digits. Kawachi him-self answered after just two or three rings.

Conscious of the couple within earshot behind me, I kept my voice as low as I could. 'Hello, Kawachi-san? It's Fujino . . .'

He replied unhurriedly, 'Fujino-san . . . Which Fujino-san would that be?'

'Oh good, so you're there. Can I come over? I'm calling from a friend's place.'

I looked around at the others. The man had his eyes lowered and was munching on a strip of dried squid.

'I haven't seen you for days. I'll be right over. Ten minutes, tops. See you!'

I replaced the receiver. I picked up my daughter, who was sound asleep, and said to our hostess, 'I'll be on my way.'

'You sure you're all right? You're fairly drunk, you know,' she said doubtfully, half rising.

'No problem. The night is young.'

The man guffawed. I smiled at him and exited. The cold air felt good on my sweaty body. Further down the street I became nauseous and crouched above the gutter with my daughter still in my arms.

Kawachi was the only one who knew of my lie, and after that day I couldn't stop being intensely conscious of him. Because he half reminded me of my humiliation, he was hard to miss. But I'd fled like a coward on those occasions when I actually caught sight of him at daycare.

Now my voice was vibrant as I gave him directions on the phone. I hurried to change back out of my pyjamas and set out glasses and a bottle of whisky in the six-mat room before he arrived. Then I ran down the stairs, rolled up the shutter at the entrance, and walked towards the station to meet him.

'It's very good of you to go out of your way like this. I live on the fourth floor of this building. Through here – after you.'

After ushering him into the six-mat room, I realized I hadn't set out water and ice. As I detoured to the kitchen, telling Kawachi to make himself at home, he took a seat on the tatami and lit a cigarette.

'I'm sorry I'm not able to help out at all at the centre, I really appreciate all you do . . . I'm on my own, as you know. I don't even have time to tidy up this mess . . . I admire your wife, she copes so well, on top of teaching . . .' I kept up these remarks as I took the ice out of the refrigerator. With a smile, Kawachi looked across at the laundry hung up to dry indoors.

'You seem so well suited to each other, I envy you,' I went on. 'And it was you we have to thank, wasn't it, for arranging the funds to enlarge the playground and put in the new heating? . . .'

I headed back with a bowl of ice cubes in my right hand and a carafe in my left, but my foot caught as I stepped out of my slippers at the edge of the tatami and the ice scattered all over the floor.

'Oh, I'm such a klutz,' I said as I crouched and began retrieving the cubes one by one. It took time. I'd heaped the bowl with two trays' worth and some had slid surprisingly far. They chilled my fingertips, and the more I rushed the harder it was to get hold of the little cubes.

I suddenly looked up at Kawachi. He was gazing vacantly at me, smoking. I thought of how I must appear to him. That brought me to my feet, sending the laboriously gathered ice skidding back across the floor.

'Well, don't just sit there. Did it never occur to you to give me a hand? You've got a nerve. I think you'd better leave. I suppose all that flattery was going to your head, but really! You couldn't have picked up even one? Why did you come here?'

He stood up with a grimace and headed for the door without a word.

I watched him go, completely at a loss. That wasn't what I'd wanted to say. The ice didn't matter. What was he doing here? I ran after him and took hold of his arm. And as he turned, I threw my arms around his neck.

'Don't leave like that. Please stay . . .'

When I woke in the morning, Kawachi had already gone. I checked the time: if I didn't get up immediately I'd be late. I went from the six-mat room where I'd slept with Kawachi to the bedroom I shared with my daughter and lay down beside her. She rolled over in her sleep, turning her back. I closed my eyes and fell asleep again.

There was somebody knocking. My daughter got up and went to the door, while I pulled the quilt over my head without surfacing.

Shrieking, 'It's Sensei! Mommy, Sensei's here!' she gave my head a joggle.

'What a fuss! Who's "Sensei"?' Rubbing my eyes, I peered towards the entrance. There stood one of the daycare staff.

'Oh, you're in bed? Are you unwell?' she asked quickly, blushing. 'It's just that you've been late a lot recently, and then this morning we waited and waited and when we didn't hear from you, the director and I were worried . . . Will you be taking the day off?'

'No, I was about to, er . . .'

'I see. Well, then, your daughter can come with me. They may not mind at your office, but please make sure you're on time at the centre. It's important, not least for your little one . . . Come along, I'll take you today. Everyone's having their ten o'clock snack by now.'

Between us we got my daughter dressed and she set off excitedly. I locked the door behind them, then called in sick to the library. The new netting cast a bluish hue inside the apartment and made it feel smaller. An insect cage, that was it: until that moment I couldn't think what the newly circumscribed view reminded me of. I snuggled back into the futon left down in the six-mat room. A trace of Kawachi's odour seemed to linger there.

As I surveyed the net over the window, before I knew it I'd dropped off again.

In my sleep, I wandered into some dunes. The wind – so

strong I couldn't keep my eyes open – was blasting my whole body with sand. There I was, surrounded by sand as far as the eye could see, and all I could do was marvel at the vastness of the dunes. If the force of the wind was any indication, they went on forever. It whistled far and near.

The sand was flowing at my feet, and for want of anything better to look at I watched it. It struck me as odd: however hard the wind was blowing, surely it didn't explain that rapid flow? Then the sand whirled up momentarily into a mound, before it blew away, leaving something small and white. It could have been a newborn's head. As I bent down for a closer look, another buffet of wind caught me and I covered my face against the sand's sting. A clear, high voice rose from near where I was standing, sounding to me like *ah-eeem hee-ere*.

When the wind shifted, I searched the nearby ground for that half-glimpsed head. There was nothing there but a flat stretch of sand, with eddies whipped up by the wind streaming across its surface.

That call sounded again a little way off: *ah-eeem hee-ere*. I was sure now that it wasn't the wind. I heard it behind me too. It rose straight into the sky and faded wanly. Next thing I knew, the dunes were filled with the calls.

'Is that children?' I asked of no one in particular. A man's voice answered me:

'Those are the children who appear from the sand when

the wind is up. Which is why all they can do is raise those cries. They cry out for a while, then die. They can never leave here or make their presence known.'

'They're not suffering?'

'No, they are simply crying out.'

'They have beautiful voices,' I responded softly, then drew a deep breath.

RED LIGHTS

I awoke convinced I'd overslept again, much to my despair:
this time, there'd be no getting out of it. The narrow eyes of
my boss at work dwelled on me, as did the eyes of the daycare staff who looked after my daughter.

When I shakily went to sit up, I found a young man sound
asleep with his soft cheek nestled against my right shoulder.
On my left, my daughter too was breathing evenly with her
arm flung across my stomach. All three of us were half
under the quilt that covered the foot-warmer table.

In the dark room the TV murmured, turned down low,
and from further off came a burbling of water on the boil. I
remembered that I'd kept the kettle on in the kitchen since
morning to warm the apartment. A cold snap had arrived
with the rain the night before, but it wasn't cold enough to
drop everything and get out the gas heater. Though I'd had
no outings in mind even if it had been fine, it was so gloomy
indoors that we'd need the lights on all day, and on a Sunday
too, I thought dejectedly. So when young Sugiyama came to

see us not long after noon, I was even more overjoyed than my daughter.

Sugiyama's hair smelled of shampoo; I stroked it lightly with my left hand and closed my eyes again. The way nightmares vanish and anxieties evaporate when you open your eyes is one of life's pleasures, I reminded myself. I was in a state of contentment. I could sleep as long as I liked. There was no one there who was entitled to point the finger of blame. I tried to remember the dream I'd been having when I woke up.

I was standing in the middle of a dark expanse that seemed to consist of soft mud. I could see the horizon, beyond such wastes of black mud that I could have walked for days without the landscape varying. And there was a plane, or what I took to be a plane. I must have flown in.

Little by little, my travels came back to me. The dream had begun in a room.

Twenty or thirty people were assembled in a dim, high-ceilinged room. It held rows of long desks, four or five people seated at each. They were a motley group, not unlike the occupants of a hospital waiting room. In the diffuse light from a single large, clear window, they were reduced to grey shadows. But they all seemed to be people I knew well.

Then news reached us that there was no longer any hope for a certain person who had gone missing. I felt my body dissolve in grief. The room was hushed. I saw pale laments rise like smoke from each of the shadows and begin slowly to curl.

I left the room. I had a feeling there was something I had to do. I must hurry, I thought, and promptly found myself installed in a small vehicle. I gripped the steering wheel and depressed the accelerator. With perfect smoothness, the vehicle rose three feet off the ground and began to glide at breathtaking speed. I was thrilled to realize it was a plane, but once it reached that altitude it steadily accelerated without climbing further. Thick branches pressed menacingly in on both sides, blocking the light of day so that the narrow road ahead was virtually a tunnel. Steering frantically, I navigated its twists and turns. Tree trunks bore down and streamed away behind me.

Then I popped out into the black expanse. For a while the plane proceeded full speed ahead, but gradually it was dragged down by the mud and nothing I did – whether I floored the accelerator or rocked back and forth to jerk us forward – could regain the lost speed. Finally we stalled and the fuselage half buried itself in the mud.

It came to me then that I'd been searching all along for the person whom there was allegedly no hope of finding alive. My search seemed also to mean that I'd thrown in my lot with his or hers. I took another look at my surroundings: so I was going to die here, was I? The plane had sunk out of sight. There was nothing here but black mud. Why had I been so drawn to that person? I must have wanted something, I thought, racking my brain. Whoever was it? My quarry was probably somewhere in that sheet of mud, watching me . . .

This was Sugiyama's second visit to my new apartment. He'd also visited maybe a dozen times during the four years I lived with my husband. For the first two of those years, Fujino had been giving him private tutoring, when he was an undergraduate himself and Sugiyama was in high school. I could still picture him clearly as he was then: pale, fleshy but delicate, and too timid to look people in the face; he was at the bottom of his class. This didn't stop his father, a professor, wanting him to go to a prestigious university, and he was prepared to pay for all the tutoring and cram schools it might take. It's ridiculous, Fujino used to grumble to me. The taciturn boy seldom raised his eyes; Fujino could speak to him as bluntly as he liked and receive only a shyly smiling nod. It annoyed me, his grovelling like that, no matter how bad his grades were or how unprepossessing he might be, but I tried to protect him from the things that made him behave that way. I took pleasure simply in getting him to act his age, to relax and smile at one of my jokes.

After a year of cram school, Sugiyama had passed the entrance exams for a not-long-established private university I'd never heard of. A year or so later, he'd confided in Fujino that he couldn't keep up; the tuition was a waste, he wanted to drop out and find a job. Fujino had roared with laughter and told him he really was beyond hope. Sugiyama had reddened and lowered his eyes. That day, I dragged him off to see a movie. Then, at twenty, and now, at twenty-three, he still had the soft contours of baby fat, and he never drew himself up to his full height. When I separated from Fujino, he was one of those to whom I sent my change-of-address postcard.

On his first visit to my new apartment, Sugiyama had given no sign of noticing that all trace of Fujino was gone. He arrived with a cuddly toy rabbit he'd bought for my daughter. And he was at her command with piggybacks and wrestling matches; he even took her down to the neighbourhood playground. When he was leaving, she gripped his hand and wanted to go with him. As I picked her up, letting her scream, Sugiyama's own expression was torn between laughter and distress.

As we were about to say goodbye, I told him I was no longer living with Fujino. 'It's just the two of us now,' I said. 'Come and see us sometimes, if you feel like it. I mean it.'

He nodded earnestly. For all my enthusiasm, I wasn't counting on his actually showing up; I was well aware that in my present unattached circumstances, any man anxious to stay on the right track would steer clear of me. By the following Sunday, I'd forgotten about Sugiyama.

But he did turn up, in the rain, carrying a big bag of groceries. The moment I saw him on the doorstep, I practically shrieked to my daughter, 'Quick, it's your friend from the other day! Come here, quick!'

He had bought vegetables – bok choy and spinach and the like – and chicken. He set to work intently, with my daughter underfoot and me chattering away. When he was done, the dish was a chicken stew, though from the colour I'd have guessed beef. We sat down together to try it at once, along with the dinner rolls he'd brought. It was so good I had to laugh out loud. I ended up having three helpings, spluttering with laughter at Sugiyama's expression. My daughter too kept holding out her little bowl for a refill, her forehead beaded with perspiration.

Once the big saucepan was empty, we grew sleepy and lay down to watch TV. My daughter was soon fast asleep, sucking the edge of the quilt that covered the *kotatsu*. For her sake I turned down the TV and switched off the overhead light, then returned to my spot between the two of them.

'It's siesta time,' I said.

Sugiyama smiled just as he used to in high school. The sight made me turn and pull his plump body close, then bury my face in his chest.

'That's comfortable, like resting on a cloud . . .'

'I'm fat, that's why,' he answered ashamedly.

'It feels very nice. There, I can hear your heartbeat clearly . . . Did you know the heart is the first part of the human body to develop? . . . First the heart, then the head and the spine.'

'Are you sure?'

'Yes, I'm pretty sure that's right . . . Want to listen to mine?'

Sugiyama nodded and pressed his ear to my chest.

'Can you hear it?'

'Yes, I can . . .'

'It's the same, isn't it? . . .'

We both fell silent. I closed my eyes and tried to catch the sound Sugiyama was listening to, that of my own heartbeat. Before long, I sank into sleep.

After seeing Sugiyama off at the station in the early evening, we stopped in at a bookstore, where I bought my daughter a children's magazine that came with an assortment of free gifts. What I'd been told by the daycare staff was still weighing on me: that she had slipped into the infants' room next door while their backs were turned and had been caught on the point of trying to cut off a baby's earlobe with scissors. The four teachers and the head of the centre had detained me for what seemed like hours, and they'd had a great deal to report: she often kept to herself in a corner, she had little appetite for lunch, she bit other children and pulled their hair. In short, to my mind they seemed to be teaming up to

persuade me that my daughter was a bloodthirsty little monster capable of killing a peacefully sleeping baby. They
looked at my little girl's face and they saw a bloodied baby. In
their eyes, my child's hands and face were red-soaked.

I'd wanted to block my ears against the sound of my own
voice, so loudly had I raised it in the staff room, while the
chair I was gripping scraped the floor. I'd started by exclaim-
ing they couldn't possibly be serious, obviously she'd simply
been holding a pair of scissors when she'd taken a peek at the
babies and was about to pat one on the cheek, forgetting
what she had in her hand. But by the end I was bowing my
head deeply and begging them repeatedly, on the verge of
tears, to give her the benefit of the doubt.

It was true that she'd been changing since I'd erased her
father from her life. But I was prepared to believe this meant
she was becoming keenly alive. The pleasure she took in
even small things was heightened now, and she savoured it
avidly. Maybe I needed to get used to the idea that, to an
outside observer, those changes might give the impression
that she was capable of taking scissors to a baby and creating
a bloodbath. I wanted her joy receptors to be even more finely
tuned. It was because the system wasn't yet fully formed that
she often cried. Her daily joy intake ought to leave her so
knocked out that she would sleep soundly at night.

I was buying her the magazine, then, because now no
chance to offer her moments of joy seemed too small. I'd
never bought her a decent toy myself, never mind a magazine.

Her father used to buy her toys – too many, in fact – and I'd thought of it as his job.

With me bearing the magazine in its paper bag, we dropped into a café for a fruit juice for my daughter and a coffee for me, then headed for the apartment. On the way we had to take an overpass and then cross at the traffic lights. My daughter gripped the overpass railing to view the trains coming and going below us. I stood back, holding my umbrella over her, and watched the feet of passersby on the bridge. They all skirted a large puddle in their path – until one child's red boots jumped in with a splash that wet not only his legs but mine. The mother's voice could be heard scolding.

From under the umbrella, I recognized these two. It was Kawachi's child, two years older than my daughter, and Kawachi's wife, whom I saw occasionally at daycare. She'd been shopping, judging by the supermarket bags. Recognizing me too, she dipped her head with a smile. Behind her stood Kawachi, glowering at me in embarrassment. I returned not his wife's greeting, which I ignored, but his look, adding a touch of derision. A tumult of expressions played across his face. His cheek muscles twitched as his wife looked wordlessly first at him, then at me. Almost at once he turned away, took his child's hand, and briskly passed me by. As he went I spoke the single word 'Hah!' His wife looked back at me, loathing unmistakable in her face.

Kawachi had spent a single night with me – and only then

because I'd begged him to. There didn't seem to be any good reason to hate him. We'd both acted out of a physical desire that shouldn't be that difficult to forget. I'd got naked and held him tight, and with a smile on his lips he'd lain on top of me, or placed me on top of him, and moved his pelvis. When I awoke in the morning, he was already gone.

He hadn't been back since. As he chaired the daycare parents' association, I would see him around the centre about once a week. When we ran into each other, he spoke to me in the same cordial way as before, urging me to attend their next meeting.

It would have been better if he'd pretended not to notice me on the overpass.

Watching his hastily retreating figure, I felt a sense of relief, as if a weight had gone from my shoulders. I felt compensated. So now Kawachi was aware for the first time of the hate he had inside him, and it was because of me. He would continue to detest both me and his own carelessness for having spent a night with me.

I didn't know who was more guilty, the one who invited or the one who accepted, but I didn't think there was much difference. In any case, I couldn't miss the fact that Kawachi's smiling affability towards me had been tinged with pity. So let him go pity himself.

We ran towards our building, my daughter and I, sending up great splashes on purpose. Even her hair was spattered with black mud. Hooting with laughter, she scooted along in the rain-swollen gutter. I circled ahead and leaped out at her with a lavish splash. She sat down heavily, then rolled about in the muddy water, helpless with laughter.

I closed my umbrella, took my sodden daughter in my arms, and walked on slowly in the rain.

Another week of the daily round between daycare and the library began.

My biggest fear at that particular time was sleeping late. More often than I liked to remember, it had been well after ten when I came to. I'd received repeated warnings, both from my supervisor and at the centre. As I went on meeting these accusations with hurt looks – it wasn't as if I meant to sleep in, after all – I came to think that maybe everything would be forgiven if only I stopped sleeping in. Forgetting my other troubles – my daughter's behaviour at daycare, how to get my husband, Fujino, to consent to a divorce – my one fear was sleeping in. It was because I overslept that Fujino had it in for me and my daughter was being assessed as a problem child. Nobody would see me as a reliable mother.

When I did manage to get up on time, the boost it gave me lasted all day. And on the days when I was running late I dashed down the street on the point of tears, swearing at my daughter instead of at myself.

It had been a day of this kind when the train I took in the evening hit a suicide. I'd reported for work at almost eleven, and my supervisor, Suzui, had got to his feet with a disapproving sound. I braced myself for whatever was coming, but he just sat down again.

So when I heard other passengers exclaim that we'd stopped because someone had jumped in front of the train, I remembered my late start and cursed myself: see, this is what happens. The first three cars had entered the station when the train came to an abrupt stop. Figures went sprinting down the platform, while on board everyone fell quiet.

After a while, passengers from further back began moving forward, passing from car to car. I followed suit and entered the next compartment. Those pressed for time, together with would-be sightseers, were leaving the train through a door that must have been opened by an impatient passenger. I was in a hurry myself as it was nearly time to pick up my daughter. But I approached the steadily growing group midway down the platform and stood there, unable to see, but gripped by a sense that I shouldn't distance myself from the person who'd gone under the train as if it were nothing to do with me.

What burden of suffering or grief had brought them to this point? How long had they spent on this platform, and what were they looking at? They'd stood here alone, unnoticed. Now there was a whole crowd staring at the cast-off physical body, mangled and bloodied. What pain had driven them to it? I wanted to know, I badly wanted to know.

Silver-suited ambulance attendants descended to the tracks, carrying a stretcher. Shivering, I edged in among the crowd. I was afraid, and would have liked to bolt. But I felt the person staring at me. In response, I moved forward, step by step.

I reached the front of the crowd after the stretcher had been removed. Fresh red blood was pooling between the tracks. I bent forward for a closer look at the scene, while fighting the urge to retch. A single yellow sandal, a woman's, high-heeled, was lying about fifteen feet away.

Just then, the train started to move. I fled the spot on shaking legs, not glancing back. Who are you? I wondered.

Another week passed: it was a Saturday afternoon.

I had picked up my daughter from daycare and was ambling homewards with plenty of pauses for chasing cats, observing the progress at construction sites, and playing a kids' pachinko machine in front of the bakery.

Our route included a quiet slope flanked by a fine old house and some apartments. There were red splotches on the pavement, a vivid red. I studied them as we made our way up the street. They were overripe berries dropped from an idesia tree.

When I lifted my face to the sky, the berries in their grape-like clusters gleamed an opulent red against its blueness.

At the edge of the pavement, where the tree's large leaves had drifted into piles, my daughter threw one up in the air. The dead leaf barely became airborne before falling softly back onto the berries. I took a turn at flinging the same leaf towards the sky, which was a deep, dazzling blue.

THE BODY

I was ten minutes early for the session. I entered one of the row of waiting rooms and sat down on a bench. In a corner were seated two greying men who were consulting documents from black attaché cases they had open on their laps, while behind me sat a young man, with a little girl of perhaps two in his arms, and a young woman who was pregnant. The only sound was their murmured conversations.

I hadn't expected to find myself in this place. I tried to commit the details to memory as if what I saw were a scene in a dream. A scene constantly on the point of altering or melting away. This flimsiness surely meant it must be concealing some surprise that one would never guess beneath the surface. Every time I heard footsteps coming down the corridor, I held my breath and raised my face. It was never my husband, Fujino. Wouldn't you know it, I thought, and returned my gaze to the other people in the waiting room.

In my mind's eye I was vaguely sketching my own demeanour if Fujino did show up – what I should say, how I should look. Would I start by producing a deeper bow than necessary and thanking him formally for going out of his way to attend? Or could I carry off greeting him with a nostalgic smile and the words 'I'm so glad you came, I was afraid you wouldn't'?

I overheard the young man holding the little girl say, 'Don't worry, it seems the mother is nearly always granted custody.'

The child's cranky voice interrupted with something I didn't catch. Then the woman's voice continued, 'But it's up to you in the end. Because this little one and the new baby mean the same to me: they're both my children.'

'I know, I know. Haven't I practically been a father to her?'

'That's what's got me worried. He dotes on her – men do, don't they?'

'So just say she's mine too . . .'

I had applied here in person about two months ago, but then completely forgot having taken that step, so that when the notice arrived I was mystified. I puzzled over the postcard, wondering why I'd received it, even though the word 'mediation,' when I'd first heard it from Suzui at the library, had been enough to send me scurrying, acting on his advice – or, no, of my own accord – to the building where I now found myself.

The men in the corner went out together, and through the same door a short middle-aged woman stuck her head in and called my name. I hurried into the corridor, where the woman, who was checking the adjacent waiting room, said in a hushed tone, 'Oh dear, he doesn't seem to have arrived yet. What shall we do? Have you heard anything? We've not had any word from him.'

'I haven't either . . . I'm sorry.' I bowed my head, at the same time clenching my fists: so that meant Fujino might appear in this corridor and spot me at any moment.

'Well, why don't you come into the mediation room, all the same? He may well join us still.'

'Certainly.'

Since I dreaded meeting Fujino in a place where I wasn't prepared, I hastened ahead of her to the room I had been assigned. Its numbered door was one of those lining the left-hand side of the corridor; the waiting rooms lined the right-hand side. Numerous waiting rooms were apparently required to allow the parties not to come face to face while they waited.

The woman opened the door and ushered me in. Sunlight – almost too much of it for the poky room – was streaming through the windowpanes. One person was already sitting behind a large desk, where the woman who had fetched me now joined him, seating herself in a black swivel chair. She invited me to sit down and make myself comfortable. Smiling amiably at the older man, I chose one of several chairs placed haphazardly in front of the desk.

'Is the other party not here yet?' asked the old man.

'Evidently not.'

'It's five past. I do wish people would be on time.'

'I'm awfully sorry,' said the middle-aged woman. 'I'm sure you're very busy.'

Stammering, I added my own apology. The old man addressed me:

'Well, there's nothing for it but to wait a little longer, as we can't start unless both parties are present. We're expected to wait thirty minutes.'

'Oh. I'm so sorry.'

'Although if he did show up half an hour late, we'd have our work cut out. There's the appointment after this one to think of, you see . . .'

'That's right,' said the woman, 'you were handling . . .' They resumed a desultory conversation, not looking at me. After ten minutes, she stepped out to look for Fujino and returned alone.

'If you ask me, he's not coming,' said the man.

'You might be right. I wonder what's keeping him? He could at least have got in touch,' his colleague sighed.

'He won't come today. If they would only tell us in advance, we'd waste a good deal less of our time like this. These cases are most frustrating.'

I bowed my head to them both again. So Fujino wasn't coming. I might have known. I recognized that all along I'd been bearing in mind, with a hint of hope, that he wasn't likely to show up in a place like this. And at the thought of that probable no-show Fujino actually showing up, there was a catch of apprehension in my breath. It had been decided, however, that he wasn't coming. The moment I was certain of this – more certain than the two people in front of me – I felt my body gently relax.

'Rather than wait for him here like this, would you prefer the waiting room? I'll call you again when the time is up.'

Returning hurriedly to the waiting room, I sat down on a bench, my legs sprawled in front of me, and lit a cigarette. Five minutes passed, then ten: no Fujino. By now I wanted to get out of that building just as soon as I could.

I was called once more to confirm my intentions: 'It's a pity about today, but will you leave your petition standing?'

I nodded without hesitation. Now that I'd tried once to summon Fujino, I could only keep on trying. Whether or not this was all a dream.

'Very well. One has to be patient. People who are summoned tend to take a good while to respond. It can sometimes take a year or two. When shall we make the next session?'

I noted the agreed date and time in my appointment book and left the room. I closed the door, walked a few yards slowly, then broke into a run. I couldn't stop myself. For the first time that day, my legs were trembling.

From then on, I expected to hear from Fujino. Not having shown up at the mediation session, he would try to arrange to meet me somewhere else. Or so I'd convinced myself.

Christmas was over and the year was drawing to a close.

My daughter was eagerly awaiting the New Year festival while happily reliving Santa Claus's visit to her daycare and his patting her on the head. When she talked about her father, she had taken to calling him 'Old Daddy.' This was her deft way of working around her mother's aversion to the word 'Daddy,' and once she'd hit on it she started telling me the memories she had inside her. I listened noncommittally. She talked about her father as if describing someone her mother wouldn't know. Speaking of a trip to an amusement park as if it had been just the other day, she was full of enthusiasm: 'You should get him to take you too. Don't worry. I bet he will.'

Fujino's phone call came on the library's last day before the holidays. We agreed to meet the following day in a coffee shop. Neither of us mentioned the mediation.

The next day was the last day of daycare. After taking my daughter there in the morning, I dropped in at the hairdresser's for a shampoo and wave. Back at the apartment, I put on makeup and, after much indecision, a dress I'd bought after he and I separated. When I was ready, I phoned my mother and asked if my daughter and I could come over the following evening and spend the New Year with her. She agreed, her tone seeming to imply that there could hardly be any other way of spending the holidays, could there?

The previous year, I had stayed the nights of January 2 and 3 with her. It was the first time I'd spent the night there since I'd gone off with Fujino and moved out. But I had chosen that stay to tell my mother that we were separating and I was setting up on my own. After putting my daughter to bed, I invited my mother to join me in a whisky and, while picking at a marinated salmon delicacy she'd prepared, I reluctantly broached the subject. Fujino had urged me to do it during the New Year.

When we returned to our home, he'd greeted me with relief; he'd thought I wouldn't be back. During the month that followed, I neither went to see my mother nor phoned her – not until Fujino had left and my daughter and I were installed in our new place.

I couldn't immediately find the coffee shop he'd named and was a little late for our rendezvous. He was seated by a window. As he caught sight of me he half rose and smiled, his face flushing as he did so. My own smile was equally ill at ease.

As I'd anticipated, he began by mocking me for resorting to mediation. 'That's for people who have property worth fighting over, it's no place for someone like me without a penny to my name. I'm sorry, but I can't even afford child support. Surely you know that?'

I nodded, then explained what had led me to apply. I'd wanted to be sure that our consent to divorce was truly mutual, to avoid complications later. Ideally, of course, we'd talk things through between the two of us, but I for one would become emotional, and all in all I had a feeling we'd never get anywhere without a third person present; besides, I felt it might be best to have an official record of what we decided. All this I explained in my defence. As I spoke I glanced around the interior of the coffee shop that Fujino had chosen, trying to gain some sense of his present life. The chairs were dark red leatherette; the walls were patterned with intertwined foliage in a strangely vivid green.

We'd had quite a number of rendezvous in coffee shops before now. The ones where he'd always asked me to meet him were near my work or in my neighbourhood. Sometimes, late at night, I'd had no choice but to bring along our sleepy daughter. But these conversations always took the same course. Each of us started out meaning this time to close the gap even a little, ready to share the blame, hopeful that the situation might still resolve itself naturally; and, instead, one of us would soon take some casual remark amiss, and once we stumbled it was all we could do to protect ourselves from each other's emotions. Fujino would lament and curse at how I'd changed: whoever was that woman he used to know? And I would fall silent.

That day, too, the words 'official record' set Fujino off – 'Do you trust me so little?' – and we seemed about to go down the usual route.

'You're the one who can't be trusted, if you ask me. You think you're on to a good thing taking it to mediation, but what if I told them what you're like as a mother? Suppose I told them how you led on a guy like Sugiyama, who was a student of mine? What do you think would happen? I'd get custody, I guarantee you that.'

How could he have known about Sugiyama? With a shiver, I replied, 'If that's what happens after there's been a proper discussion, then so be it.'

'Oh sure, when all you care about is not losing her.'

'Yes, of course I do, but you feel the same way, don't you? If she goes to you, though, you've got to tell me where and how you plan to bring her up.'

'You haven't told me anything.'

The colour was beginning to rise in both our faces.

'What more is there to tell? I'm just carrying on with the life you know. Nothing's changed. I get up at the same time, I pick her up at the same time from daycare. What has changed . . .' I broke off.

'. . . is you,' he said.

I shook my head.

'Anyhow,' he went on, 'the fact is I can't take her, so there's no argument there. I can't even pay what I owe you, let alone child support, so I have to see things your way. But I can't stand how you take advantage of that. I would love to take her, if only I could, and I bitterly regret that I can't. You don't know how it feels, do you? That's why I at least hoped that, together . . .'

His face twisted and his voice grew tearful. This was going to end like all the other times. I took the plunge, though I felt my strength desert me: 'Oh, I know . . . At Christmas, how I

133

wished we'd worked things out enough to spend the day together, the three of us . . .'

'Oh come on, knock it off. It's you who won't let me near.'

At that moment, Fujino absolutely hated me.

At Christmastime I had got out the little artificial fir tree from deep inside the closet and assembled and decorated it with my daughter. That tree, its tiny lights twinkling. Her, motionless before it for a long time, rapt in its multicoloured drops of light. And me, standing back, looking on. To her, it was the most beautiful of sights, countless joys shimmering invitingly in their splendour. It was a cheap tree that Fujino had bought at a local supermarket when she was a year old, saying, 'This'll do for now, won't it? It'll only get broken with her touching it. They're really quite expensive.'

'You've gone for the cheapest, by the looks of it,' I'd teased as I admired the tree.

Now I said, 'It's true, I really did wish you were there . . .'

He turned his face away.

'. . . I want us to work things out as soon as possible so that we can have a nice time together, say every Sunday, if we decide on Sundays. That's all I care about . . . I don't really understand why we can't. But . . . you have eyes only for your daughter, you don't see me at all. I think that's what gets me, and I don't want to let you see her . . . I'm afraid to . . . If only we could just meet up and have a laugh and not have to think. I don't want to be constantly thinking, "Where does this leave me?" You can be how you want, I don't care who you are, as long as when we get together we can all have a nice time . . . I've never asked you for anything, have I? I don't need anything, believe me. But . . . you look at me and you're thinking only of your child. And that's what I can't take. Can you understand? . . . That's why I'm asking you this one thing: to wait until everything is settled formally before we arrange visits. I'm not saying I'll never let you see her . . .'

I fell silent and hung my head. My hands, in my lap, were shaking as if stimulated with electrodes. Fujino appeared to be saying something, but I didn't hear. I was revolving one thought in my mind: if only he'd forget the past, that was all it would take. As simple as that. Since we'd been living apart, as time passed I'd ceased to be able to associate the husband I used to have and Fujino as he was now. That was the change in me.

After a while, he got up and left. I sat there a little longer.

I thought back over the Christmas Eve I'd spent with my daughter a week earlier. I'd picked her up from daycare in the evening and, without coming home, we'd taken the train three stations along the loop line to a department store. As it was after closing time, we rode the elevator straight up to the twelfth-floor restaurants. Every one of them was crowded, this being Christmas Eve. Yet the crowds pleased me. I wanted their company. We weren't the only ones, my three-year-old daughter and I, living in this city.

After I'd dropped quite a few hundred-yen coins vying with my daughter in the game arcade on the same floor, we tried a Chinese restaurant. They had no table free; we would have to share. The other occupants were two fiftyish women who wore showy earrings and rings. My daughter took a look across the table at their faces and her high spirits suddenly sagged.

My energetic 'Well now, we're having a treat today, what would you like?' met with a flat 'Anything' as, head down, she raised only her eyes to me and answered in a small voice. My jolliness gradually became too much of an effort, so I sipped my beer, my idle gaze filled with the comings and goings in the busy dining room.

Although I was prepared to take my time now that we were there, my daughter had barely picked at the special meal when she started to insist on going home.

'Have a bit more. It's good, isn't it?'

'I don't like it. I want to go home.'

'There's nothing to eat at home. Eat up now or you'll get hungry.'

'I've had enough. Let's go. I hate it here.'

'Do you? I like it.'

She lost her temper and dashed her half-filled plate to the floor, where it smashed loudly.

'What a thing to do, you naughty girl!'

The scolding set off a wail that carried through the whole restaurant. 'I wanna go home! I wanna go home!'

I had to pick her up and make a hasty retreat. Once outside, by the time I stopped in front of the elevators she was smiling and eager to get down and roam. Exasperating as this was, while glowering at her attempts to squirm free I thought that, all the same, we were the only two people who wanted to go back to that apartment.

When we started down the main street after getting off the train, this time she announced she had to do number two.

'We're nearly there, hold on. I can't do anything for you here in the street.'

I hurried her along, pulling her roughly by the hand. But she sobbed at once, 'I did it!'

As she was too discomforted to go a step further, there was nothing for it: I found a spot out of sight, took off her underwear, wiped her bottom, and put on the clean pair I had with me. When I straightened up with a sigh, I saw a man coming from the direction in which we were bound, staggering as he walked. As my daughter and I watched, he collapsed and let out a sound that echoed in the street: weeping or moaning, I couldn't tell.

'That man's crying,' whispered my daughter, gripping my hand tightly.

'He feels bad, he feels awful,' I whispered back.

'Make him better, Mommy.'

'Me?'

She nodded, not taking her eyes off the shadowy figure in the road.

I looked at her and bit my lip, then I threw the dirty underwear I had in my hand into a nearby garbage pail and went over. An odour of vomit was in the air. My daughter's lapse had also left a lingering smell in my nostrils, and I felt a touch of dizziness. I crouched beside the figure.

I began to stroke the back of the quietly groaning sufferer. The man was just a drunk, but his back was broad and hot. The body was a solid one. Its ears were so red, they seemed about to catch fire. My daughter reached out too and we stroked together, four-handed. He wore neither coat nor sweater, having apparently wandered out of doors from somewhere. Intent on stroking the stranger's back, I found myself drawn into a kind of fervour, as if praying for a miracle. It seemed we were stroking for a long time, but it may have been a matter of moments.

We were so absorbed that when the back stirred and the body righted itself, it took us completely by surprise. The man had got to his feet. Open-mouthed, we watched him go. He hunched his shoulders painfully and tottered off towards the station, and we never even caught a glimpse of his face.

'He got better. He was feeling awful and now he's better,' my daughter murmured. She seemed pleased.

I pulled her to me and took a deep breath. The smell was still rank. 'Thank goodness.'

Hand in hand, we set off. Our hands felt glowingly hot from all that vigorous rubbing.

I noticed a number of stars twinkling in the sky and

exclaimed, 'Stars!' The colder it is, the more clearly they appear: that was the thought that came to mind.

After the New Year, I took a seat in the mediation room again. The same faces were there across from me, beside each other. I waited ten minutes, a quarter of an hour, gazing at the high-rises I could see through the window. The sky was blue that day too, and the mediation room was warm and stuffy.

THE EARTH'S SURFACE

I stayed on the train. It was a Sunday afternoon. My daughter was not at my side.

At first, I kept count of the stations each time the train stopped – four, five – as if building a tower of toy blocks, but after a while I knocked it down myself.

I tried to adopt the attitude that I'd meant all along to travel for hours, but I still felt ill at ease, convinced that, any moment now, somebody aboard the car would detect that I had no business being there. I felt uneasy being observed by the other passengers as I just sat, turning over in my mind the obvious fact that unless I made a move and got off, the train would carry me to an increasingly distant destination. I had no interest in going anywhere, I had merely settled in, grateful for the warmth from the vent at my feet, putting on a very weary air and thinking lazily, 'Not just yet, not just yet.'

The older woman to my right had dozed off, her head lolling on my shoulder. More than her head: her whole weight slumped against me. A gentle push with one hand might have woken her or at least made her shift, but I went on tensely supporting her weight. It was surprisingly hard work to keep my own body from tilting sideways. We might both have had a more comfortable time if instead I'd leaned towards her, nestling my head on hers and snoozing in a twosome like a mother and child. But I looked the other way and scanned the pages of the sports paper that the man on my left was poring over.

In letting the woman rest her weight on me I was hoping to escape my own uneasiness, if only a little. Like the woman's, my own body had weight accompanied by warmth, and this steady reminder of it was not without a certain sweetness.

Once, in my early or mid-teens, I too had dozed off on a stranger's shoulder on the train: not the usual wobbly nodding off, but a deep, refreshing sleep. It was only when I was eventually woken by a tap on the head that I realized my pillow had been my neighbour's shoulder. So that was why I'd felt so good: there was a moment's letdown on finding the cause was so simple. When I struggled upright and looked him in the face, stammering an apology, I was met with a grin of obvious amusement. In the middle of my muddled apologies the young man stood, smiling, and got off the train. As my gaze followed his departing back in the knowledge that he must have been aware of my body, through its weight, for some time, I felt a self-consciousness and an attachment that were akin to love.

I could no longer recall his face or how old I was at the time; that rush of emotion that made it hard to breathe was all that came back to me now.

When I was still a child, the same emotion used to haunt my dreams.

At the time, I had not yet taken in the reality of my father's death. I understood that I would never see him again in this world, but because there was a room at home that was just as it had been when it was his, I thought he was still present, even if he wasn't visible to my eyes. I had entered the world at more or less the same time as my father departed it.

In my dreams, I often sneaked into that room. A man sat on the floor, his back to me. At times he sat on a futon that appeared to be left out permanently; at others, he sat bleakly in the centre of the empty room. I would timidly approach his back, cling to it, and lean against him with all my weight. Sometimes this would cause the man's upper body to topple sideways, impassively, like a doll. Or he might sit stonily no matter how hard I leaned. Occasionally, though, I succeeded in obtaining the reactions of a live person. Warmth and softness would communicate themselves to me as I leaned against him. His back would give a little under my small weight. And he would start to turn his head towards me.

At that moment I would wake, unable to bear whatever was coming. Terror dimmed my sight and robbed me of strength. That man must never have a living body, not even in a dream. We who were alive were not allowed to meet revenants from the dead, for in the very act of sensing their warmth we yielded that which was most precious to the living.

Seized by fear, I would have an overpowering sensation of spiralling down into dark nothingness. That was without a doubt my worst nightmare as a child. But even as it petrified me, it was so intensely pleasurable that I couldn't help feeling guilty. That supposedly inaccessible warmth and softness delivered a joy as sharp and dazzling as a lightning flash, and I couldn't tell the fear and the joy apart. I was around four or five at the time.

Sugiyama had not shown up that Sunday either. I had grown so accustomed to his Sunday visits that, although they'd only lasted three weeks, I couldn't remember what our Sundays used to be like without him or think how to spend the long hours with my daughter. It was no use waiting, since he hadn't promised and I hadn't confirmed that he'd be around that week. No phone call in the morning meant he wouldn't come. University final exams were on, and if Sugiyama wanted to graduate he most likely couldn't afford to fritter his time away with us. He might not be very busy, but he must need a Sunday to himself every now and then. Maybe he'd feel like playing with my daughter when he was free again. It would be enough if, when he did, I welcomed him with a smile as if he were an impulsive kid brother.

Considering his age, though, there was always the worry that we'd seen the last of him, that he'd never give those Sundays at my apartment another thought. For a student like Sugiyama, there were all too many things out there to run across for the first time. I owed the Sundays he'd spent with me to the fact that, at nearly twenty-three, he was still sheltering in the parental nest and hadn't even found himself a drinking buddy of his own sex.

The three of us had gone to the supermarket together, cooked up our 'specialties,' played at shadow tag and chain tag in the park, gone on aimless walks, and even taken a trip to the zoo. But it was when we simply lay around the apartment that we were in the most perfectly relaxed sync. My daughter would climb onto Sugiyama's stomach, or conversely have his head in her lap, and she'd sing him a lullaby or tell him a story, then get him to read to her, or order him to sing any song he knew. He would keep her company drowsily as I watched from under drooping lids. Sometimes, we taught her the games we knew from our own childhoods, competing to explain how to flick *ohajiki* or slap down *menko* cards, play statues, and rock-paper-scissors with the feet . . . It was as simple as that. Once or twice I'd put my arms around Sugiyama, but only so we could nestle sleepily together.

He always came around noon and left before nightfall.

The previous Sunday, I had expected him all day. I left a note and hurried back when I took my daughter shopping, but there was no sign of him, just the note still taped to the door. While the washing machine was running, and when I was up on the terrace hanging out the laundry or in the toilet wiping my daughter's bottom, I kept an ear out for a knock at the door. Tiring at last of the wait, I blew up at my daughter over nothing, and as the afternoon wore on she let herself out of the front door in an attempt to escape my temper. Caught and dragged inside, she started to bang her head on the wall and scream, and when I lifted her in my arms she had a fit of rage, blotches of purple mottling her pallor, her teeth grinding. I said goodbye to my remaining hopes of seeing Sugiyama again and laid her down on the tatami, cooled her chest, and, once the bout subsided, took her out for a walk.

These infrequent fits of rage had started in the New Year. Most of the time she was, if anything, readier than before with a seemingly carefree smile, and though she was still crying in the night, her appetite did seem to be picking up little by little. And then came these frenzies of rage, triggered by what seemed to me oddly trivial complaints. I took her to see a doctor, who gave me a prescription, and meanwhile I also consulted the friend who was a nurse at a university hospital and the mother of a daycare classmate; our two families had often got together when I was still living with my husband. I was sure my daughter couldn't have had a tantrum at daycare yet or I'd have been told. I was thankful for this much. Even if the staff there were to find out, Fujino must not know. I was in the midst of the process of summoning him to attend divorce mediation, without a response so far. The third session was a month away. In the meantime, I wanted to do anything I could to soften the grip of the rages that seized her.

Even if Fujino had nothing else to say in the mediation room, he would certainly question me about our daughter's health. And I would answer shortly, 'She's fine.' I therefore wanted to do what I could to lessen the anxiety I'd be struggling not to show at that moment. Clearly, if Fujino ever got an eyeful of what was really happening, he'd take his accusations against me to an entirely new level, clasping his poor little girl to his chest with great reluctance to let her go, and he'd be in and out of my apartment all the time. I wasn't blameless, and I'd even have to accept frequent visits if Fujino's putting his arms around his daughter would help free her from her rages. However, I had a strong feeling it would only add to them. Now that his life revolved around new relationships, all he could do was give his daughter a proprietary squeeze now and then while protecting that separate life and making me yield to its demands. He could not have taken our daughter in, nor could he return to live with us. That he might reflect on whether he'd contributed in any way to his daughter's rage was too much to ask. Pity, that: I found myself feeling cheated on her behalf.

The nurse had been informed by Fujino that we were

separating, at a time when I wasn't yet able to take him seriously. 'Stay in touch,' he'd told her. Dumbfounded, she'd asked what he meant, and glowing with renewed youth he'd explained, 'It's simple: I move out and I go and visit them, let's say on Sundays.' When she inquired about finances, Fujino said he wouldn't be in a position to send support for a while, considering he was hard put to earn even his own keep, which was what had led to his decision in the first place.

She'd told me later that she couldn't make head or tail of all this, but had somehow found the presence of mind to say: 'You're taking an awful lot for granted. That'd be a really sweet deal, anybody with children would jump at it. I certainly would, if I could come and go as I pleased and everyone was happy about it. But it doesn't work that way.'

She'd reported this exchange to me at the time, and now that I had to explain my daughter's tantrums to her, nearly a year later, it was heartening to remember what she'd said.

A few days after I consulted her, she told me she'd asked the advice of a specialist and some senior colleagues and had given the situation some thought based on her own experience, and this was what she proposed until we could think of something better: why not bring my daughter over to her place every so often? Nothing special, of course: they'd simply let the children play together, and maybe they'd all go to the public bath, and she could stay for dinner. Luckily our daughters already got along well at daycare, mine had been to their house before, her hosts would actually be glad of the chance to let the girls entertain themselves, and one way or another it couldn't do any harm.

I hesitated to accept, protesting in a small voice, 'But she already gets enough playtime at daycare.'

'It's not the same as around the house,' said my friend.

She thought my daughter's problem was having to be on her best behaviour too much. Let her spend some time in home surroundings where, unlike at the centre, nothing would be expected of her and, who knows, she might settle down, because she was after all just a little child. And one couldn't be sure, but maybe time away from her mother wouldn't hurt either. It wasn't a question of good parenting or bad. Maybe she just needed a chance to unwind . . .

My daughter began staying overnight with them once every four or five days. According to my friend's reports, she certainly wasn't homesick. In fact, she was so lively it was difficult to get her off to bed, she called my friend 'Mommy' and the husband 'Daddy' with no sign of embarrassment, asked for whatever she wanted, and would even push their own child aside to climb onto 'Daddy's' shoulders or lap, and there'd been only one night when she'd cried.

Gradually, in my eyes too, their house had come to shine more brightly than the others on their street.

Thus, the day I'd brought on one of my daughter's tantrums when I grew tired of waiting for Sugiyama, my steps turned in its direction of their own accord. All smiles the moment she realized where we were heading – the speed and obviousness of the transformation were astonishing – she started tugging my hand, shrilling, 'Come on! Faster!'

Although we showed up unannounced at their door, in the end they offered to take her for the night, and after dinner (for which I was easily persuaded to stay), I returned alone to the apartment. So great was the sense of relief that flooded me at their house, I couldn't bring myself to decline anything out of politeness.

Sugiyama didn't come the next Sunday either.

I kept telling myself that I was *not* going to get my hopes up this time. My daughter had spent Saturday night with the nurse's family, and I thought that arrangement was proof positive of how little Sugiyama's visits meant to me. By Sunday morning, however, my ears were again straining for footsteps on the stairs, a knock at the door. More than once there really was a knock and I flung the door open, my pulse racing. It was the newspaper-money collector or someone selling mutual-aid society memberships.

At midday, I phoned to check how my daughter was doing. That call ended with the nurse advising, 'She insists she doesn't want to come home yet, so try again around two.'

After dawdling over my weekly housecleaning, I phoned again. There was a pause while the sound of my friend cajoling, mingled with my daughter's crying, came from the receiver, then it was picked up again. 'She won't hear of it. What do you want to do? We've got nothing on this afternoon and it's no trouble at all to have her here.'

I replied hesitantly, 'Then, I'm sorry, but would you mind if she stayed a little longer?'

'Very well, try us around five o'clock.'

I shoved my wallet into my coat pocket and left the apartment. My exasperation with my daughter was making my head spin. Weirdly, I caught myself resenting her – a three-year-old – much as I might resent some sort of overseer. I was well aware of why she was in no hurry to come home, but still I was idiotically breathless with hurt: how could such a little child turn against her mother?

I headed for the nearest station, bought a ticket and boarded a train, intending to go to the big supermarket one station away. Once plumped down in a vacant seat, I didn't get up at the next station, or the one after that.

The woman sleeping with her head on my shoulder woke with a start and scrambled off at the next-to-last stop without a backward glance, and I finally made a move at the end of the line. I saw by the station clock that it was not yet three.

The town was in the neighbouring prefecture, overlooking a large harbour. I'd been there once before on a school trip. Even from the platform, the masts of some of the ships were visible.

I left the station and, asking directions as I went, made my way to a spot where I could view all the ships in port. As I walked empty-handed and in sandals, I enjoyed feeling that I could have passed for a local resident.

I arrived at a park situated on high ground. The harbour lay beyond it to the left. I stood at the railing at the point where it was closest to the water and began to observe the ships at their berths, one by one. I counted six big foreign vessels and two small ferries. There was also an outward-bound ship with a pink hull, but it was obscured by haze – a sea mist, perhaps.

My eyes came to rest on that indistinct pink shadow and I watched it gradually dwindle. It was a subdued tone of pink, a pink so pale that it seemed detached from the surface of the sea, which gleamed like sheet zinc.

As I watched, the shadow shrank to a point, then dissolved into the flat light of the sea. I gave a shiver and let out the long breath I'd been holding. I took another look at the foreign ships at anchor but I'd lost interest in those other boats. The pink dot was still floating in my field of vision like an insect.

With my back to the harbour, I surveyed the park. On spotting a payphone I rushed over to it: it seemed to me now that calling had been on my mind all along.

First, I phoned Sugiyama's home number. His mother answered and passed me over curtly to him. He greeted me vaguely, perhaps cautious about his mother overhearing.

I launched into what I had to say: 'I know I shouldn't have, but I'm calling just this once because if I don't say this now, I never will. Listen, you want to clear out of there, don't you? I can tell, I've known you since you were in high school . . . So I've been thinking. I don't expect you to start fending for yourself straightaway, I know it must be especially tough with an inferiority complex like yours . . . But don't stay there and let them treat you like a fool or you'll become one . . . You don't owe it to them to stay, and you can't expect them to protect you forever, even if they are your parents. They've been hurting you since you were a child, they've gone to great lengths to hurt you and now they can't leave well enough alone. Parents are just parents, there's nothing special about them. Sometimes you just have to cut your ties, you know? And don't let anyone tell you otherwise . . . So, for a start, why not come and live with us? You can rent the little room on the eastern side. I'll feel more secure that way, and she'll love your company. You'll be helping us out, I'll only ask for a nominal rent. Actually I'd make it rent-free but I don't want to make you uncomfortable . . . Come on, it'll be fun. Think of it as communal living. We can do it. Seriously, we'd make a great team, you and me . . . So think it over. The room's there, anytime you like . . . Well, what do you say? . . . You might never have a chance like this again . . . When are you coming? . . .'

Sugiyama said, 'I'm sorry, the idea doesn't interest me,' and hung up.

After glancing up at the flat light on the sea's surface, I

next dialled the nurse's number and had her put my daughter on. '. . . It's not time to come for you yet,' I said, 'but I just had to tell you something . . . Are you there? It's a ship. Yes, a *ship* . . . A pink one. I saw it just now. Really. A pink ship. It was a long way off . . . Next time let's come and see it together, I bet you'll think it's great too . . . It was a ship like the one we should be on, you and I . . .'

Each time I paused, I heard my daughter clearly encourage me to go on. There were no other voices or sounds in the background. I felt as though everything except my daughter had vanished at the other end of the telephone. I pictured her, bobbing there all by herself on the surface of the sea, using both hands to hold the receiver, which was too big for her, and to press it to her ear.

The physical distance between us allowed me a pillowy kind of peace. As I continued to speak down the line to her, tears came to my eyes.

FLAMES

That evening, on the way to collect my daughter from day-care, I encountered yet another funeral. It was on the street I always took from the station, inside an eye clinic where I used to go myself. Floral wreaths flanked the entrance of the old, low building, and from the open doors black-and-white curtains receded into the interior. There was no one on duty outside; perhaps the service was over.

The clinic had belonged to a dour old doctor. He had seemed to have no assistant or nurse, nor many patients. His office contained a jumble of medicine boxes, and its floor was on a slight incline. The funeral was most likely his, but perhaps not. Much as I would have liked to go in and ask, I didn't even pause outside.

I was encountering a lot of deaths. I've lost track of exactly how many funerals I came across on my regular routes; it surely can't have been all that many and yet, at the time, I couldn't shake the feeling that deaths lay in wait for me at every turn. And I couldn't help wondering what in the world they were trying to tell me, appearing like that, one after the other.

The weather was unsettled at that time of year, on the cusp between winter and spring. Some days brought a warm, moist wind that gusted from morning till night; others brought an inch or two of snow. It was a season when those who were ill were liable to slip away. My apartment was in an old neighbourhood where many households were elderly: I supposed that was bound to translate into these numbers. The local death rate that year had nothing to do with my having moved to the area. Why should it? Yet each time I met with another passing, my mind sought to link it with myself – to pin it on me.

The first had been at the flower shop directly across the street from the building where I lived. It was the owner who died. The neighbourhood association's black-and-white marquee went up in front of the store. The funeral was a big one, with many wreaths. The store reopened in less than a week. My daughter and I remarked that the middle-aged woman – evidently the florist's daughter – who now stood in the open storefront had red rims to her eyes, as though she'd been weeping moments before.

Then it was the old retired barber who lived above his shop next door to our building. For two days we had to thread our way among the easels holding floral wreaths on the sidewalk as we came and went.

It was when I noticed the next funeral, at a house near my daughter's daycare, that I thought with a ripple of alarm, 'This is going too far.'

But there were more to come. Kobayashi, my former boss, died not long after that. He had been in the hospital for the better part of a year with cirrhosis of the liver. Suzui, who had replaced him when he took sick leave, broke the news to me one morning as I arrived at the library. Suzui attended the funeral that day, bearing a condolence offering with my name accompanying his own on the envelope. On his return in the late afternoon he told me it had been a good, simple funeral. But Kobayashi's domestic situation had apparently been complicated; there'd been two women present who could have been Mrs. Kobayashi, and Suzui hadn't known whom to approach or how.

Even Kobayashi's death didn't particularly affect me – or, at least, not with sadness. There was an intervening layer of surprise and fear. I was starting to sense some obscure intent in this string of deaths.

And I continued to encounter still more funerals, days apart.

It was right about then that I was laid low by flu. Having felt unwell since I got up in the morning, by evening I couldn't stay on my feet in the kitchen, and my temperature registered over 102. For a start, I lay down with my legs under the foot-warmer quilt in the tatami room and consulted my daughter: 'Mommy's sick. I can't do a thing ... I'm wondering what to do about you. Shall I call Mitchan's house and ask her daddy or mommy to come for you, so you can stay over, like you always do?'

About once a week she stayed over at the home of a playmate from daycare. Mitchan's parents had talked me into this, initially to let my daughter have some breathing space, but gradually both she and I had come to count on these breaks. My husband, Fujino, had not responded to my third request to attend divorce mediation. His phone calls and letters had ceased, and he no longer showed himself in my daughter's vicinity. All signs of him seemed to have vanished from my life. One could call this a peaceful time, I suppose, but in fact I spent it on edge with something close to fear, because I no longer had any clues as to what to expect. In response to her mother's tension, my three-year-old daughter was having frequent fits of anger.

She took with alacrity to spending nights away, right from the start. The anxiety was all on my side, and more than once I woke up in tears, having dreamed I'd lost her downtown. In time, though, I came to sleep deeply on those nights when I had the whole futon to myself, and I'd even begun to prompt her, 'How about going to Mitchan's tomorrow?' She needed no coaxing; she'd give a squeal of delight and start singing 'Mitchan's tomorrow, Mitchan's tomorrow' to a made-up tune.

When I'd ask her if I could pop in, she'd answer excitedly, 'You come too, Mommy. We can eat dinner together.'

Which made me feel like joining in her song while doing a little dance.

When I found I was running a temperature of 102 degrees and would be out of action for at least a day, my thoughts automatically turned to Mitchan's family. My mother lived not far away, but I couldn't let her know. I hadn't even told her how things stood with Fujino. I wanted her to think everything was swell and my daughter and I were positively blooming. My attitude to my mother was like my attitude to Fujino.

'It's OK, I won't go to Mitchan's, I'll stay with you. You're sick, aren't you, Mommy?'

That day, her face entirely failed to light up at the word 'Mitchan's.' In surprise, I pressed her: 'Are you sure? It's *Mitchan's*? I might not be able to take you to daycare tomorrow. You'd have to stay home all day.'

'I don't mind. Mommy, are you sick?' She peered at me as she repeated the question. She seemed fascinated by the idea. I nodded, took her hand, and put it on my forehead.

'It's hot. You're really sick.' Her eyes sparkled. She went on to touch my cheek, my lips, and my hand, her expression showing signs of growing excitement.

I got up and gave her some bread and milk and cold sausage, then burrowed into the futon that I'd left down in the two-mat room and was asleep before I knew it.

I woke in the night to find a cleaning cloth on my

forehead, dripping wet, and my daughter, still dressed, curled up asleep on top of the quilt. The lights and the TV were on.

We stayed in all the next day. I dozed, and she wiped my face with a towel, took my temperature, and brought me glasses of water, which she poured into my mouth and onto the tatami; she also watched TV and napped contentedly, her head pillowed on my arm. We sipped rice porridge – invalid food – together. And that night she too ran a fever – nearly 104 degrees. It was my turn to minister with damp towels and mop her perspiring neck and chest.

The next morning, my own temperature being down to near-normal, I took her on my back to see the doctor, who gave us both medicine. I knew I should at least stop to buy milk and eggs, but we came straight home and, after taking our respective medicines, went back to bed.

The following day, her fever too began to go down at last. But she had developed the diarrhoea that always followed a bout of illness. I put her in a diaper, long outgrown; even so, the futon and her lower body didn't escape soiling. The room was oddly cosy, filled as it was with our own warmth and the smell. Washing her diapers, which took me back, I fell into a stupor as if still feverish myself. But then it occurred to me that it was Saturday – I had a day off ahead, no permission required. The fridge had been empty since the previous day. In the evening, while my daughter slept, I did the shopping. In addition to milk, eggs, and vegetables, I bought bananas. I remembered how, when she was a baby, I used to scrape a banana with the rim of a spoon and carry the mush to her mouth. I couldn't remember how big she had been at the time, though.

That night, I freshened us both up for the first time in three days, using hot water from the kitchen. First I sponged my daughter's face, neck, and hands, then her chest and back. Then, holding her down with my left hand as she squirmed ticklishly, I gave her lower half a thorough sponging. After changing the water, I took off my top and began to sponge my neck and arms with a hot towel while she watched. When it arrived at my chest, she reached out timidly to touch my nipples. I paused and watched the movement of her hand. She tweaked a nipple, then instantly pulled back in hoots of laughter. I had already hunched up with unexpected ticklishness, covering my breasts with my arms.

She rolled about giggling on the futon, then lifted her face. 'Can I do it again?'

After a moment's hesitation, I nodded. She took my nipple between her fingers, holding on this time and pressing harder, trying to squash it.

'Ow! Careful, you'll break it!'

I pulled away from her hand. Rather than pain, I was overtaken by chills. As a newborn baby, her sucking had sent the same chills through me: a shudder accompanied by a keen joy.

'Does it hurt?' she asked, eyeing my nipples uneasily.

'Well, of course. And if you break them off, they won't grow back.'

I quickly put my pyjama top on, flustered in case she'd noticed the sudden chills.

'Yes, they will,' she said. 'They'll come out again.'

'No way. And neither will the milk.'

'Is it all gone?'

'That's right. You used to drink lots, though . . .'

'I want some.'

My daughter's eyes were sparkling again.

'You can't. I told you, it's all gone.'

I stood up and escaped, laughing, into the kitchen. But once I'd put the lights out and we were both in bed, she reached out towards my breasts again and said, in a voice that held laughter, 'I'm a baby . . .'

'Aha. So you are – you're even wearing diapers.'

'Mewble mewble, mewble mewble.'

I had to laugh. 'That baby has a funny-sounding cry. More like a cat, I'd say.'

Breathless with stifled laughter, she went on: 'Mewble mewble, my tummy's hungry.'

'Wow, so this baby can talk already?'

'Mewble mewble. Want mommy mook.'

'There, there, hush now. It's all right, then, here you are.'

I pulled her to me with a grand gesture, tugged my top up to uncover my breasts, and pressed her face to my nipple.

She closed her mouth around it for a brief moment, but then started laughing shyly and took her mouth away. She left her cheek resting on my breast, all the same, and was soon sucking on the edge of my pyjama top instead. She never could go to sleep without a bit of cloth to suck, since she'd been a baby.

Towards daybreak, I had a dream.

I was on an outing, some sort of school picnic or factory tour, with a couple of dozen other people. These seemed to be classmates from my elementary school days, but they had grown up and were adult size.

We were being kept waiting for something on the landing of a drab staircase in an office building. Some drank soft drinks, some excused themselves to go to the bathroom. Thinking this was my chance, I began to change my clothes.

Next thing I knew, I was surrounded by shocked looks. I glanced down at myself, only to discover my right breast showing through a gap in my underwear. Startled, I tried to conceal it, but couldn't.

A voice snapped, 'What do you think you're doing? Shame on you!' There was a chorus of remarks: 'Put your clothes on. Now!' 'That's what you get for dithering.' 'How embarrassing!' 'What a place to choose.' 'Talk about clueless!' 'She's such a loser.'

While fumbling away, I was thinking sadly that they were right. Why hadn't I found some more secluded spot? I'd simply thought I could do a quick change while nobody was looking, but now what was I to do? My underwear and blouse had got all tangled up and I couldn't tell where the sleeves were or where to put my head. I'd probably have to take everything off before I could finish dressing. The more I fiddled about, the more my right breast showed itself.

The thought that I was not only upsetting everyone but would get left behind reduced me to tears.

A man gave my back an encouraging push. 'There's plenty of time, silly, why don't you go to the washroom? I'll follow you.' On shaky legs, I started to climb the stairs.

There was no one in there. My escort found a chair in the washbasin area and sat down, turning his back. 'Make it quick. There's no one here, you're OK.'

He was an old classmate whose name I'd forgotten but whose face was very familiar. From behind, he looked just like a bigger version of the child he had been.

'Very well.' Relieved by the quiet, I began undressing. I would be naked from the waist up, so I thought I'd better say something, and told the man, 'Don't look.'

He laughed. 'I'm really not that interested.'

'No, I suppose not.'

Reassured, I stripped to the waist and set to work untangling my blouse from my underwear. My arm brushed the man's shoulder; his skin was soft to the touch. Now that I looked properly, he too had nothing on. Though he was full-grown, his back was as smooth as a plump child's. Every time I moved, my hand or back or nipple brushed against his skin. I held my breath, bewildered by this turn of events. Everything before my eyes went dark except our skin, which had begun to glow. Though on the verge of screaming in fear, I was lost in wonder at those luminous skins . . .

On waking in the morning, I noticed that my nipple was still a little sore. I glanced at my daughter asleep by my side and found myself taking a deep breath as the succession of deaths came back to me.

I was back at work at the library when I had a call from Fujino for the first time in three months and met him in a nearby coffee shop. He was letting his hair grow long.

He asked how I was; I answered I was very well.

'You want a divorce, right?' he continued. 'Are you going to insist on getting the family court to mediate?'

I nodded.

'For crying out loud . . . If you want a divorce that badly, let's get it over with. I just think it's a shame we couldn't have talked it over like reasonable people. It's exactly a year since we split up . . . and I've had enough. I'm worn out.'

I stared at him, stunned. I had been growing vaguely resigned to the possibility that I might end up still married to Fujino. However, I told myself not to believe him yet. He was a man of many moods.

But he had more to say that day: 'It's been tough on me too, toughest thing I've ever dealt with, but it was me who left, I guess, so I can't complain . . . Take good care of our girl. Let's discuss the arrangements another time. Don't worry, you can have custody. I couldn't do anything for her anyway . . .'

With a wry smile, he drew a paper from the inside breast pocket of his jacket and handed it to me. It was the divorce form I'd sent him in the autumn. I had already filled my section out; now Fujino's side was also completed and bore his seal. The witnesses' section remained blank. 'You file it,' he said. 'I'll leave it to you.'

'. . . But, are you sure?'

These feeble words were all I could come out with. It was so sudden. I couldn't take my eyes off the paper, and meanwhile I had lost all sensation in my body.

'Am I *sure*? Isn't this what you wanted? I'm doing what you wanted, that's all.'

'. . . Thank you.'

Without being fully conscious of it, I had bowed my head. I wanted to put the same question to him again and again: was he sure, might we be making a huge mistake? I had indeed wanted a divorce all along, and yet, flying in the face of those wishes, I had an urge to huddle up to him and cry, 'Maybe we've got it wrong – weren't we hoping for something different?' All I did, though, was sit in front of him, my head lowered, in a daze.

Before he left, Fujino did some explaining: he wouldn't be able to repay the money he owed me for some time yet; he meant to pay child support when he was able to, but this too was impossible for the present; he didn't want to let people down by abandoning his dreams of making a movie and creating a small theatre company. He got up to go.

'Sorry to call you out while you're at work.'

I murmured, 'No, *I'm* sorry,' with another bow of my head.

He paid for our coffees and disappeared from my sight.

So it was true, then? I remained seated for some time, unable to move. The magnitude of what I was now certain to lose was overwhelming. Whatever our relationship may have been like for the past year, he was, after all, the man who had been closer to me than anyone else. The only man I'd ever wanted to share my true feelings with. I hoped he at least understood that I was entirely without hate or bitterness towards him. He might have felt the same way, for all I knew. I could only think that perhaps there existed a kind of bond that required both parties to believe themselves hated by the other. Both Fujino and I were flesh-and-blood human beings who didn't want our lives to end yet.

The thought left me even more drained of strength.

By now, the weather had turned consistently warm.

Late one night, I was woken by a loud boom. The building rocked. My daughter woke too, calling out tearfully. My heart was racing as we went up onto the rooftop terrace together to see what had happened. I scanned the streets: nothing looked unusual. But I could see people leaning out of windows here and there; clearly I wasn't the only one to have heard the explosion.

I searched further, hugging my daughter's head to me as she continued to cry with fright. What on earth had made that noise?

Suddenly, a shock that seemed to send cracks through our bodies hit the building, accompanied by a sharp flash. I shut my eyes and ducked involuntarily, then resumed the search. A much louder boom than the one I'd heard in my sleep resounded in the night; at the same moment, the sky flared red. I still had no idea what was happening, but the beauty of the red glow that spread and intensified as I watched took my breath away.

There was another blast and a new red glow lit the night sky. By now I'd forgotten my fear. The entire sky had a sunset tinge; a shower of sparks glimmered, and to the right a burst of light surged like an animate thing, while around it the sky was flushed with the lingering glow of the second explosion. The streets too were reddened by the sky.

A fourth and a fifth explosion followed, a little smaller, then everything fell quiet. The array of colours, however, was growing in complexity and beauty.

'Instead of crying, how about having a look? I've never seen such a pretty sky. It's fantastic.'

I tilted my daughter's face up to the sky.

'Ah! Mommy . . .' Though still clinging to me, she gazed open-mouthed. The tear stains on her cheeks were reflecting the red light.

Once the blasts died down, the colours gradually faded, beginning furthest from where the explosions had occurred. Although we waited, there were no more to come, and the sky steadily darkened.

We stood on the roof until the sky returned to its original colour. We were both shivering.

In the paper the following day, I read that a small chemical factory quite a distance from our building had exploded due to spontaneous combustion, causing several fatalities.

It occurred to me that the glow in that night's sky had perhaps signalled the last of the deaths that had been happening around me. People had died in that light. Died in an instant, I didn't doubt.

I had the feeling that I finally understood what the series of deaths had been trying to tell me. The light of heat, of energy. My body was fully endowed with heat and energy. I couldn't help but see myself standing there last night, transfixed by the glowing red sky, never sparing the approach of death a thought.

CORPUSCLES OF LIGHT

Around that time, whenever I regarded the building where I lived from the opposite pavement, I would look up first at the windows of my own fourth-floor apartment, then shift my eyes to the window immediately below, which was covered by a large placard with the words 'To Let.' Only then would I feel I'd found what I was searching for.

That notice was the most eye-catching feature in an otherwise unremarkable exterior. If anyone did give the narrow office building a second glance they might be taken aback by its extreme narrowness, but its dull square windows and its walls were the same grimy colour as those of the little old shops on either side, and to passersby it was not even obvious that it was four storeys high unless they stopped and looked up. Viewed at a slight remove, the one thing that might advertise the presence of something taller than an ordinary two-storey house was the sign on the third floor. This didn't mean that the words 'To Let' registered on people passing in the street, however. Yellowed by the setting sun that bathed it day after day, the sign looked like a permanent fixture, not to be taken down regardless of the actual state of occupancy.

I was convinced that the perpetual vacancy must be in some way due to the sign. I could think of no other reason why the third-floor studio alone should go unwanted. There was no rumour of a death and nothing especially unfavourable about it compared to the other units. Now that almost a year had passed since I took up residence, I'd actually come to feel more at home in the place downstairs than in my own apartment.

At night, the building was deserted apart from my daughter and me on the fourth floor. When I went down and lowered the shutter at the street entrance after checking that everyone downstairs had left, it was as if the walls and floors that until that moment had fussily subdivided the interior turned transparent and the whole building became one great space through which a voice would echo. I felt like I had the run of the place, but in actual fact, as in the daytime, I had access only to the stairway and the rooms I rented on the fourth floor.

When I first discovered that the vacant studio was unlocked I felt a pang of childish apprehension, as if I'd personally caused something unthinkable to happen. And, indeed, once the building was shuttered, that door put me in mind of the word 'magic.' In the large, square, empty room onto which it opened, the darkness was tinged with the glow of the street's mercury lamps and traffic signals and neon signs, filtering through the paper over the window.

From then on, I visited the room downstairs many times, though never for long. I did so with bated breath despite knowing that my daughter was sound asleep in our room above and nobody passing in the street would ever have noticed my presence. Not that I felt any qualms as far as the owner was concerned. The thing was, I was unduly fond of that room, considering it was nothing more than part of a cramped, dilapidated, dismal office building. I couldn't breathe normally for excitement, and I didn't know what to do with myself; I'd maybe pace to and fro in the bare room and lean close to the window for a peek outside, and by that time there'd be goose bumps on my arms, my head would be starting to ache, and, unable to stand myself in this state, I would flee to the fourth floor. Then, sitting in my apartment, I would recall the colours of the soft light suffusing the empty studio downstairs and feel more attached to the place each time.

The windows of every floor above street level were identically shaped. It pleased me to think that, outwardly at least, the apartment I rented and the empty one downstairs could trade places and nobody would know. At first I used to worry about the studio being taken, but as the months went by the words 'To Let' found their way into my heart. The place had to stay empty, for my sake. I'd begun to pretty much rule out the possibility of a tenant. And so I would come down to earth with a jolt when I remembered that it could go any day, to any Tom, Dick, or Harry who spotted the sign and showed up at the realtor's. I could resist the idea all I liked, but at some point 'my vacant room' would be let. Having it permanently vacant was surely annoying to the owner.

More than once, the question crossed my mind: if somebody else was going to come along and treat the place as theirs, why not rent it myself? The move down one floor should be easy enough, and while the studio was admittedly intended as an office, it shouldn't be especially difficult to live there with my daughter. It was half the size of our existing apartment, but that actually appealed to me.

A room empty but for faint dancing light. If I could have had my choice of where to meet the years with my daughter that stretched ahead, I wanted it to be lying sprawled at ease right in the middle of such a room. I'd get rid of the curtains and the kitchen table. Anything I might keep about the place to make it more hospitable – even a cushion – risked causing my daughter and me pain. These days she was going for sleepovers here and there, as the fancy took her, and I was getting out and about too, in the hope of striking up conversations with strangers. We spent quite a few of our nights like this now. And yet we never forgot about each other, each of us wanting, more than ever, to find joy in the other.

I couldn't help thinking that that empty room was the perfect place for us to sleep.

In the spring, a year and a month after life with my daughter began, I received a document from Fujino, my ex-husband, and submitted it at the municipal office, thereby changing my name back to that of my parents, though any name would have done as well. I then created a new family register, which listed me as head of household.

It had been pure coincidence that the surname I'd had till then had been the same as the name of the building, Fujino No. 3. But perhaps it wasn't entirely coincidental after all. I knew the building's name when I was shown the fourth-floor apartment. I took a liking to the sunlit apartment with all those windows and decided to rent the place. It's possible that the building's name evoked the closeness of my ties to my husband and that I impulsively yielded to that sensation. At the time, I dreaded being away from him and the changes my life was about to undergo.

Because I shared the name of the building whose top floor I occupied, I was constantly mistaken for the owner. I used to receive utility bills for the stairwell or offices on the lower floors, and misdelivered mail. At one time there'd apparently been a moneylender operating out of one of the offices, and people seeking a loan, or who'd had a loan in the past, came all the way up to the fourth floor and knocked on my door, looking highly perplexed. There was no persuading some of these callers that I was not the owner or even a relative, I was just an ordinary tenant and it had nothing to do with me.

Perhaps in the process I grew more attached to the building without knowing it. The first thing that came to mind when I changed my name was to move out of there – out of Fujino No. 3, with its one apartment always vacant. It was only then that I realized how deeply attached to the building I'd become, as if the warmth of my body had permeated the vacant room on the third floor, each step of the stairs, even the noise of the shutter.

I began scanning the ads in realtors' windows in spare moments. I wanted to find a new apartment before the third-floor room was taken; that way, I could leave behind, intact, like a living thing, the self that was by now an integral part of the building.

My daughter spent that spring tirelessly gathering flowers. The roadsides on the way home from daycare alone yielded dandelions, sweet rocket, daisy fleabane, wood sorrel, wayside speedwell, nipplewort, white clover, shepherd's purse – more flowers than two hands could carry. Bunches of yellow, white, and blue were stuffed into her pockets and her child-sized shoulder bag. Sometimes she saved her finds in a plastic bag she was given at daycare and presented them to me bag and all. Since she pulled up whatever she could lay her hands on, at the roadside or in overgrown borders of front yards, the soil and small stones around the roots got mixed in, and the bag would contain bits of litter as well – the pull-tab of a juice can, a candy wrapper. I would pick out the least wilted flowers and arrange them in a glass.

Thus, flowers proliferated in the apartment also. To my daughter, flowers were a beautiful and strange life-form that, with each plucking, sprang up in greater abundance. She ran about like mad inside this life-form, and on walks with her I too found their profusion overwhelming. The cherries were blossoming, as were the azaleas; the spiraeas were snowy with flowers. My daughter would gather the cherry blossom petals that lay at her feet, and more would flutter down as she did so, alighting in her hair and on her body.

One Saturday afternoon, directly after daycare, we took a bus into the city centre to visit a park, inside the old moat, that was famous for its cherry blossoms. The day was windy. It had been overcast that morning, threatening rain, but around noon the sun began to break through, and by the time we reached the park the sky overhead was turning a limpid blue.

There was more of a crowd than I'd expected; a concert must have just ended at the venue on the grounds. The sakura were a little past their peak, and the embankment sloping down to the water's edge, which caught my eye as soon as I stepped off the bus, was vivid with sweet rocket and rape blossoms.

'Look at all those flowers! Isn't that great?' I lifted my daughter up on the spot.

She wriggled with impatience to be on our way. 'Quick, let's go down by the flowers.'

'If we can get there . . .'

'Come on, let's.'

'But look, there's nobody down there. It's off limits. And even if we could, it's slippery among the flowers, and we'd go splosh! The water is full of weeds, like snakes, they'll grab us and hold us under till we're dead. And even then we wouldn't float back up, we'd turn to skeletons down among the slimy weeds. I bet the bottom is covered in people's bones.'

'No, it's not. I can't see any.'

'Well, you wouldn't see them. The water's green and verrry deep.'

'. . . Is there a monster too?'

'Could be. It could be admiring the flowers from the bottom.'

'It can't see them!'

'No, but it can see yellow and pink and blue things sparkling up above, a long way away . . . So, are we going?' I set her down and took her hand.

'No-o!' she said tearfully.

'What's wrong? Come on, let's go.'

'No! I'm scared!' She froze where she was. I gave up getting her to move on and crouched at her side.

'. . . You're right, we can see the cherry blossoms well enough from here. There's no need to cry . . .'

She clung to my knees and rubbed her face on my chest. With both hands I stroked her soft back. The park entrance was in sight about a hundred yards further on. The pavement was thronged with people coming and going, but nobody stopped to look at the flower-covered embankment across the water.

I often lingered in that spot on my way home from school when I was in junior high.

Back then, some sort of government workers were housed in a row of desolate old barrack-like buildings in the area inside the moat that had since become a park. The grounds were planted with vegetable gardens and there was a communal well, already an unusual sight in those days. Although the housing must have been in use – there was laundry drying, half hidden by the buildings – I had never caught sight of anyone there. Not a soul, no matter what time of day I looked in.

In retrospect, it seems possible that I happened to see this scene during a brief period after the residents had cleared out, perhaps in some haste, but before it was turned into a park. Not long afterwards, the area was closed to the public, the works started, I ceased to care about the place, and eventually it slipped my memory.

As I crouched on the pavement now, looking down at the stagnant green water, I could picture as in a dream or a movie that spot as it had appeared back then, some fifteen years earlier: a spot clad in flowers and fruit trees, where the sunshine seemed to have congealed. It was bright and tranquil, disquietingly so. That was the sight that presented itself just beyond the historic old gate, as one stepped under it out of the avenue's din of streetcars and traffic. I used to think I must never tell anybody about this discovery of mine. No one else must know about this place that made me yearn to dissolve until I became a particle of light myself. The way that light cohered in one place was unearthly. I gazed at its stillness without ever going in through the gate.

I had passed that way just once more, a few years after the park opened; I was with a young man, at night. Then, too, the cherry blossoms were just starting to fall. I was wearing a short-sleeved sweater, in which I'd been warm enough to perspire during the day, but after dark my teeth were chattering as we walked.

I remember my companion scoffing, 'You're too impatient, it's only April, you know.' He was wearing a suit.

As we walked through the park, he had drawn ahead of me by about ten paces. We continued like this for quite some time. Every so often he would look back to see if I was still coming after him, then walk on briskly.

Near the park's exit, an old woman who seemed lost stopped him to ask directions. I paused too, keeping those ten paces between us, and watched. After first pointing the way, he perhaps feared she'd get lost again and accompanied her as far as the nearest big intersection, several minutes away, then gave her directions from there. Before setting off, the old woman repeatedly bowed her thanks. Rubbing the back of his head sheepishly, he turned and grinned at me. I approached, encouraged, and as I reached his side he muttered with a blush that he hoped she was all right.

Returning his smile, I told him what I wanted, and not for the first time that evening. 'You saw them all just now, didn't you, in the park? If you won't let me come home with you, let's go back there. Don't worry, we won't be the only ones.'

His face snapped back to its original expression. 'Forget it. I'll walk you home.'

'No, I don't want to leave like this . . . Why not? We can make it quick.'

'Listen to you . . . You don't care who it is, do you? Why don't you just go in there and yell out for a man? They'll show up in droves.'

'. . . Because it's you I want.'

'I've had it with you. It's disgusting. I'm not an animal. I'm a normal human being . . .'

'Same here . . .'

He snorted, with loathing in his face, then turned and strode off. I let him get a certain distance ahead before following him again.

We had shared the pleasures of sex soon after we first

met, and we'd been tangling ever since, barely pausing to talk. I didn't understand why he should be so repulsed by the desire that was making him act like this. I couldn't get rid of the idea that those physical sensations were all we had to share. We were just plain human beings: what more could we possibly ask of each other?

I could no longer call his face to mind. Two years later, I had started work at the library and met Fujino, who would become the father of my daughter.

She, who'd been burying her face in my lap, suddenly stood up and yelled in the direction of the flowers that filled our view to overflowing:

'Hey! You! Flowwwers!'

When she'd finished, I asked, 'Did they answer?'

She nodded confidently. Then, with a peal of laughter, she left me there and broke into a run, in the opposite direction from the park.

The following week, I decided on a new apartment. I made the move on the Sunday morning two weeks later, leaving the office building for an ordinary residential place. The third-floor studio was still unoccupied.

I set to work on the packing at the last minute, the night before, after putting my daughter to bed. There wasn't a great deal to pack, but I was still at it at daybreak. My daughter bounded from carton to carton, ecstatic at finding the rooms transformed overnight.

The apartment block was within walking distance. The day I'd gone to see the place, the previous tenants, a family of three, were in mid-move, contemplating the load they'd assembled in the front room as they awaited the truck's arrival.

The apartment block faced onto a narrow, twisting lane lined with buildings of the same kind.

The realtor who'd escorted me as far as the gate said, 'That's it there,' pointing to the second floor, and left me to go in alone. On the way to the stairs, in the area for hanging out laundry, a boy of about four sat with a bundle on his knees, watching me impassively. When I climbed the metal stairs and stopped at the door that had been pointed out, the child slipped past me and in through the open doorway, then, sheltering behind his mother's body, gave me a hostile look.

I explained apologetically to the woman in a head scarf that I'd come to see the apartment, having learned of it from the agency.

'My, they don't waste time, do they?' she said, and after loudly announcing the purpose of my visit to her husband in the next room, she invited me in. I stepped out of my shoes and onto the kitchen floor, but the stacks of boxes blocked my way. In any case, I didn't need a tour; I could see the small apartment quite well from there. The kitchen opened onto a three-mat room, and a six-mat room facing north. In the larger room, it seemed the light would need to be kept on even in the daytime, because of a green plastic panel that served to screen the window from the neighbours. The front door and the kitchen faced south but received no sun, being in the shadow of the adjacent block. It looked as though the window that gave onto the lane was the only one that admitted light.

Having taken off my shoes but then got no further, I stood vaguely surveying the place while the mother, made voluble by the upheaval of the move, gave me a rundown: they had been there four and a half years; it certainly wasn't what she'd call a find, due to the lack of sun; they hadn't got on with the fiftyish single woman downstairs, who wasn't in her right mind, pounding on the ceiling when they were walking perfectly normally, and so they'd paid her back by pounding on the floor, but if you were the timid type she might get on your nerves. On the plus side, the rent was cheap and children were allowed; that was all.

'We moved here without giving it much thought, because our son was on the way – and now look how he's grown! I don't know how we've managed with that old bat downstairs. Thinks she owns the place. If you plan on moving in, you've got to be firm with her right from the start. I'm not so sure you'd be up to it.'

'Hey, there's work to do. Get a move on, will you?'

The woman fell silent with an awkward smile at this interruption from her husband, who was busy in the next room. I thanked her hurriedly and left. On the way down the stairs, I peered in at a window whose checkered orange curtains were half drawn, but I learned nothing about the room as there were a tea cabinet and a bookshelf hard up against the panes.

No hurry, I told myself, we'll meet soon enough. And I headed back to the realtor's to leave a deposit.

Having secured the place, I went home to the apartment in the office building, which the late-afternoon sun was flooding with reddish light so bright it was almost suffocating. I stood in the entrance for quite a while, taking it all in, as if I'd already been gone for years and could no longer call a clear image to mind.

It was a calm scene. Everything in it was still.

When the evening sun was gone and the room lay in blue shadow, as it was time to collect my daughter from the neighbour's house where she was playing, once again I left the fourth-floor apartment and descended to the street.